THE TENS

A gripping psychological thriller about a cult

Vanessa Jones

CONTENTS

THE TENS

By Vanessa Jones

2021 ©

CHAPTER ONE

The white rock, which was nearly her height, loomed at her with a reflective sheen. The hollows in its side looked like eyes, terrifying and watching. Sophie could hear it laughing at her, like a cartoon character. Menacing mirth that echoed from nowhere but also all around her during a night that was as cold as it looked in the heart of the woods.

Despite the fear, Sophie strode up to it and laid her creased hand on the chalky surface, wanting to know if it was real. Her palm slipped upwards and she wobbled on her feet. She could have sworn the rock moved to spite her. Or maybe it was the sudden ferocious wind that had knocked her off balance. She dropped to her knees, as if she were at the mercy of an altar; hoping to be relieved of the haunting of that white rock.

Sophie knew she had to get out of there, dizzy with the desire to run away from the rock and the maniacal laughter. But no matter where she turned, she couldn't find any openings in the trees that were beginning to buck in the wild wind. In fact, with every blink, the army of trees hugged tighter together and seemed to circle in on Sophie. Like they were arm in arm, moving forth as one. With the wind all but drowning out the laughter, she pressed her back against the reflective rock and waited...

CHAPTER TWO

The rock nightmare was so repetitive that sometimes Sophie yearned for any other kind of nightmare— being chased by vampires or some kind of dystopian apocalypse. Regularly, she woke with a ring of sweat around her neck and a tight headache, part of the ritual of her taunting nightmare. That was always the same. Never changed. A nightmare she'd had since she was little. It started off infrequently. Perhaps four times a year when she was a teenager. Its frequency increased over the years, more so when she was stressed. But since her thirtieth birthday, Sophie couldn't escape the nightmare or pretend it no longer bothered her. Especially when it happened every single night.

Sophie liked to blame her husband for her uncurling sanity. But that was hardly fair. Especially since Alex had always been the perfect husband to her. With an almost rehearsed attentiveness, they were each other's best friends. The way he warmed up the car before she got in on cold mornings was all she needed. The way she waited fifteen minutes after they'd eaten dinner to suggest dessert because she knew he liked to have a break between the two, cupped his heart. The way in which she would swipe her thumb across his broad, rectangular forehead, made his smile widen.

Unusually, Alex had started coming home later and later from work. It was so out of character for Alex, being the morning person that he was. So one evening, Sophie couldn't fight off the unnamed viciousness that caused such friction on her senses anymore. She packed up the soup she had been stirring to hand-deliver to the office of the IT firm where he worked. Hoping it would put the gnawing in her mind to rest when she saw him there, hunched at his desk and the icy light of the screen shining on the pointy bits of his face that made her ache with fondness. She pictured his large nose tip pressing his cupid's bow down, over his incensed lips as he jabbed at his keyboard.

But when Sophie rocked up to the building and saw that his car was not there, she had to finally acknowledge the mounting anxiety. The anxiety that made her think the worst. She tried to lull it by being ashamed of having it. Ashamed for thinking the worst, subtly looking for proof wherever she could. And yet her body was screaming like it was trapped at the helm of a monster.

Relief swam through her like a melody when she pulled up behind Alex's car in the driveway, after she raced home, tilting the container of soup with her careless turning of corners. As she rushed in with the soup in outstretched hands, she felt guilty. For an uncouth and unreasonable panic. Trying her best to hide any trace of embarrassment or disturbance from her husband, she said breathlessly 'we must have just missed each other honey.'

'Huh?' He looked a little perplexed and Sophie knew she had to backpedal to bring the ground back to even.

'Oh, I just made some dinner and thought I'd drop it off to you at work. But by the time I got there, you'd obviously already been on your way home.'

'Ahhh. Yep.' He took the soup from her and became extremely interested in it, discarding his keys, with its silly oval copper keyring, on the bench. The keyring had been with Alex longer than Sophie had. She was so used to the way he circled his thumb over the sketched cross indentation, particularly when nervous or deciding on something. 'I made it in school and it's one of the only stereotypically manly things I have ever done, so I'm hanging onto it for a bit longer.' He would explain, whenever she poked fun at it.

Sophie was grateful that he made a big deal about the soup so she could continue to find ways to abate her shame, hidden under the decor of mundane evening tasks. The washing up. Emptying the bins. Throwing shoes back into the cupboard. Besides, they were textbook for each other and she was loathed to upset that with her petty neuroticisms. Which she noticed were becoming more frequent, thanks to ageing and lack of sleep. Ever since her thirtieth birthday, she'd been having the nightmares more and her sleep suffered. Which then translated into irrational thoughts and moods during the day and Sophie was gravely afraid it would all spill over into the groove of bliss that she'd created with Alex.

CHAPTER THREE

When she lifted her head from her pillow, she spotted a damp imprint and tried to rub it off. Flinging back the covers, she shuffled out of bed, leaving her sleeping husband behind.

Alex entered the kitchen a little while later in his pyjamas and looked across to Sophie who was in her nightdress and dressing gown, sipping coffee and looking forlornly across their backyard.

'Nightmare again?' Alex asked.

'Every night since I turned thirty,' Sophie replied.

'Aww, hun. White rock again?'

'Always. Are you going to be late home from work again tonight?'

'I don't intend to but you know... it's work.' Alex shrugged and accepted the cup of coffee that Sophie poured for him.

'I thought I'd take the day off. Hopefully get some energy back.'

'Painting today?' He asked her. The question

seemed innocent. But to Sophie, it was loaded. Real or imagined.

Sophie sighed and said 'I'm going to try. I feel so blocked ever since I turned thirty. Is this just what happens when you get old?

Alex laughed and hugged Sophie, 'Probably! Maybe you just need some decent sleep?'

'Who doesn't?'

'True. I gotta get ready for work.' He kissed her on the cheek and left her alone with her coffee.

By the time evening swept in, Sophie was still in her sleepwear from the morning. Worriedly checking the clock and then the window to see if her Alex had arrived home from work yet. Passing a framed photo of them happily embracing, she smiled to herself. She kissed two of her fingers and pressed them against the photo just as Alex walks in and the air becomes heavy with Sophie's suspicion.

'Sorry, Soph. Work was…' Alex rushes in, arms full of papers, his discarded tie and apologies.

But Sophie points to the backyard. 'Did you see that?'

'What?'

'Something flew across the yard.'

'Flew? Like a bird?'

'More like whipped across the yard.' Sophie's panic started to rise, especially as Alex wasn't taking her seriously.

'What do you mean? Can you talk sense please?'

'Alex! I think someone is out there. Or a large animal or something.'

'Like a bear?' Alex mocked her.

'Yes! I'm serious.'

Alex shuffled past her impatiently and dumped his keys and briefcase on the kitchen bench. 'It's not a bear.'

Sophie caught up to him and wobbled his shoulder back and forth. 'Why aren't you listening to me? I'm scared.'

'Okay. I'm sorry. I'll go check.'

'Please. But be careful. It could be an intruder. Or something dangerous. I don't feel good about this.' Sophie wiped her hand across her stomach nervously as Alex exited to investigate. He came back quicker than Sophie would have liked.

'Honestly Sophie, there is nothing out there. Are you tired?'

Gritting her teeth, Sophie said 'there may not be anything now but I swear I saw something out there. There's no way I imagined it.'

'Okay, okay. I'm not suggesting you're making it up or anything,' with the very tone that implied that he did. 'But perhaps it was a trick of the light?'

'Or, perhaps, it's some junkie about to stab us in our sleep. But sure, it's the light.'

'I know you're scared Soph but that's no reason to get mad at me. We're safe, nothing will happen! Let's go to bed, hun.'

Sophie obliged but slyly took note that Alex double-checked the lock on the door before coming to bed. As she lay in bed she stared at the ceiling whilst Alex removed his work clothes and got in beside her.

'Honey, I'm really worried about you. Things seem a little off-kilter. Maybe it's time you go to the doctor? Or have a spa day with Bree?'

'Bree hasn't returned my calls for weeks. I have no idea why she is ignoring me. Anyway, I don't know her that well. Perhaps she decided she wasn't that interested in being friends with me anyway.'

'She's probably busy. I wouldn't worry too much. Book the doctor and see what they have to say. Til then, let's get some sleep, hey?' He leant across and kissed her goodnight.

CHAPTER FOUR

A noisy cacophony of birds woke Sophie up. She groaned at being awoken by them when she desperately needed more sleep. Risking an eye open, she searched for her phone to check the time. She rolled over to discover Alex's side of the bed empty. Smiling to herself, she knew that Alex is probably up making her coffee at that very moment.

Wandering into the kitchen with the doona wrapped around her, she spies that the kitchen is empty. 'Alex? Honey?' Sophie called out. The birds finally had quietened down a little.

Shuffling over to the kitchen bench with her doona around her shoulders like a cape, Sophie reached for the folded paper on the benchtop. Picking it up was instinctive. You see a folded note, you pick it up to read. The action was so automatic that she forgot to be anxious about what it would mean. But then she read the sparse words of Alex's handwriting: 'I have to leave you. I'm so sorry. X'

Sophie gingerly placed the note back down on the countertop where she found it and unblinkingly moved to the sofa.

CHAPTER FIVE

Underneath the doona on the couch and still in a state of shock, Sophie reflexively switched from looking at the muted TV, like a zombie, to her phone to the note that Alex left. And she stayed there until it turned dark outside. With nothing more than the TV light reflecting off her. Devoid of any reasonable thought or reaction. Her memory short-circuiting every ten seconds as she forgot what she was doing and lifts the strange note in her hand to her eyeline again.

She considers calling her new friend, Bree, but something stops her from going through with it. It's the thought that their friendship is so new. So unformed. It almost felt inappropriate to Sophie to call upon her.

Sophie met Bree not long before her thirtieth birthday at an awkward group where everyone pretended they were happy and at peace with their life. Even the lady that was hiding her relationship with her first cousin. And the woman who paid for her husband's mistress's mental health treatment. And the woman who ate rubber bands. Sophie started going to the groups to get out of her head and heal herself from the nightmares. She thought that a little meditation wouldn't hurt. But the whole time she just felt like a petulant teenager that couldn't fit in. The one good thing that blossomed from it was meeting Bree and how quickly they connected. It was the way the blonde shiny woman smiled at her that sucked her in. It was also the way the fresh-faced lady was cheerful but in which Sophie caught her smile fall away on her pearlescent pink lips too quickly. Her French-tipped nails were spotless, Sophie noticed, as Bree waved them around in direct cadence with how she spoke. A simple, understated wedding band adorned a finger, which felt in stark contrast to the overtly obvious diamond earring studs and de-signer label jeans.

It was in Bree's sparkling, unhurried demeanour and the way she just let compliments somersault out her mouth that encouraged Sophie to relax a little inside; something that was few and far be-tween. Each time they caught up for coffee, Sophie found herself more and more engaged in Bree's life and warmth. And on the day that Bree referred to her as "Soph", she thought she had truly found a friend. But without explanation, Bree hadn't re-turned at least three of her recent calls. So she stopped trying. She knew a dismissal when she saw one. So Sophie continued to be held by her fugue state, alone, there on the couch trying to work out what the note really meant and if she had somehow mistaken its meaning. Perhaps Alex would simply be back after work? Maybe he meant to say 'I have to leave you in bed.' But Sophie knew. Deep down, she knew.

Once it was well and truly night time, somewhere in the back of Sophie's mind a rational thought pushed its way through, like it was pushing through a crowd. The brainwave forced her into action, the doona dropped to the couch as she stood up and stalked out of the loungeroom into her bedroom where she flung open the cupboard doors. Desperately searching for any missing items, she was perplexed that there was barely anything missing besides a bag, one T-shirt and one set of pants. All his socks still seemed to be lined up in the drawer, grinning back at Sophie.

Stomping into the bathroom she spied his toothbrush missing from the holder. But as she scoured around, she discovered it was flung into the rubbish bin, its chewed head pressed into the plastic liner like it was ashamed of Alex's behaviour. *He didn't even take his toothbrush*, she thought hopefully.

Armed with the new information, she tried to ring Alex again. And, again, it rung out. Spotting her dishevelled and utterly defeated appearance in the bathroom mirror, she hung her head over the basin and started to sob.

CHAPTER SIX

During the promise of the next day, even after a seemingly endless night of no sleep, it dawned on her that something wasn't right. Husbands do not just decide to leave. Not on an ordinary morning, without a hint of unrest. Not when they'd only recently made love with a sweetness that they each thought was long forgotten.

She still could not bring herself to phone Bree. Who knows what the additional sting of her not answering the phone would do to her in such a fragile state. But even Sophie could see that she desperately needed a friend. Unfortunately, the only ones she had were Bree. And Alex.

There really was no place to go and look for him but what other choice did she have? The powerlessness of staying home, waiting and ringing, felt like it would decay her soul. She pulled into the car park of his work, despite being told by the main reception, several times, that he was not in the office.

Sophie didn't believe her. Instead, believing it was clearly a ploy to stop her hysterics that she was bound to unleash on Alex. Regretfully, she stopped ringing his work after the receptionist tactfully suggested she stop ringing, for her own sanity as well as his. But she had to see for herself.

Feeling conspicuous in her car she pulled up directly underneath where his office window faced down over the car park. If he was actually there, he would surely see her, come down to avoid any scene or abate her irrationality. There was no one in his office, as far as she could tell. But it wasn't worth the risk of leaving. So, she waited some more. Every minute twisting at her gut. Time had stretched so much that she did not understand how it could ever go back to normal; cut into blocks, marked by normal activities like meals or the hum of peak hour traffic.

Well beyond home time, Sophia did not spot Alex making his way towards his designated car park. Which she realised now, was empty and had been the entire afternoon that she sat cramped up in the driver's seat, breathing her own fetid breath, staring at his office window.

She gives Maria, the receptionist, one last call.

'Hello, IT Associates, how may we help?'

'Hi Maria, it's Sophie. Is Alex in yet?' Her voice sounds foreign to her.

'Sophie, he hasn't been in for a few days and definitely not all day. Please stop calling.' Maria hung up on her and she felt the coldness of the phone click off. There wasn't an ounce of worry in Maria's voice. She clearly knew something about Alex's decision that Sophie didn't.

Could Alex be in danger? She couldn't think why.

The thought of going to the police made her stomach churn. The last time she was at a police station was as a child, wrapped in a stiff grey blanket. That's all she can remember of the time she lost her parents. The blanket was as unyielding as a side of a cardboard box and wrapped around her just as awkwardly.

No, she thought to herself, *the police can wait. Besides, he left a note. He wouldn't have left a note, if he was in any kind of trouble.* How embarrassing it would be to go to the police when really, her husband had just not wanted to be married to her anymore. The humiliation flicked at her like a snake's tongue.

Sophie's legs felt like cement as she mindlessly pumped them, alternating between the brake and accelerator and headed back to her empty cave all whilst coming to the realisation that he wasn't at work and he wasn't at home. The life they had weaved together started to unpick in her mind as she faced that he clearly just didn't want her anymore. Otherwise, he wouldn't have left her with such a pathetic half-assed note.

Driving home was a sort of exhilaration, the shock creating an adrenalin bomb that made Sophie was as ill as she was excitable and she giggled with the absurdity that her love was no longer her love. She deliriously giggled all the way into the shower, where she tried to strip a layer of her skin off with the hottest the shower water could get. And just as quickly as the hysteria had started, it stopped. She screamed his name into the cold, glossy teeth of tiles. The wail bounced back at her from the reflective surface and reflected back her pain. This was just the beginning of, what she assumed would be, unbearable heartache. And she was scared.

CHAPTER SEVEN

I t didn't take long for Sophie to begin to plummet. It wasn't living alone that saw her change. Sometimes she doubted it was even the fact that the love of her life had abandoned her. It was as if something greater was happening to her. Something that had been threatening to break the banks her entire life, undulating underneath the surface of her skin and she had been clever and strong enough to keep it at bay, really well in fact, until now. Emotional distress had taken off a layer of her armour and now she was exposed without an inner barricade to keep back that torrent of emotional sludge. Whatever it was, it was confusing and unrelenting and she did not know where to put it.

Sophie's senses started to shut down, one by one. Not shut down as such, just... dissolve. What they could once easily and unnoticeably tolerate, they now revolted against. An olfactory alteration first. Always a lover of scents, the mysticism and romanticism of smells transfixed Sophie. She could smell when something was cooked to its best through a deep inhale, could identify the components of anyone's favourite perfume and her life was incomplete without a scented candle burning. Although it had started before Alex had left, it came at her with full force in his absence. Petrol, perfume and certain foods were the enemies. The tang of the creamy, yet artificial, coconut shampoo that she'd used for more than a decade was too pungent and she was forced to rinse her hair in benign liquid that could only be bought at weekend sunrise markets. Even the sting of toothpaste became too much. Which threw her because somehow, as if they sensed her inner decay, her gums became tight and began retracting as fast and as far away from where they normally sat. The rate at which she was grinding her teeth down served only to exacerbate the problem. If she pushed her tongue— *had it always taken up this much room in her mouth?*— into the cushions of gum that filled the space between her teeth, a foul taste would emit, like a citronella collar on a barking dog.

Her behaviour became obsessive to curb the daily peeling back of her identity. Seven minutes exactly in the shower; she timed it. One slice of cheese, one slice of tomato, one slice of pineapple from a tin and two leaves of iceberg lettuce, all salted with a violent shake of the salt shaker. This constituted her midday and evening meal. Introducing any new items of food made her stomach curl over itself.

Her nights were filled with splotchy sleep: she took half a pill after dinner, to assure herself she'd be okay, at least until midnight when she would routinely wake up, flick on the TV and watch harmless reruns, often the same episodes so there were no surprises, no nasty little hidden plots that she couldn't handle. The sound of her TV friends would lull her into a half-sleep for a few hours, when she would wake up startled from the nightmare and repeat the process until light broke through the curtains. Morning break was the worst part of her day. At least sleep gave her hope, an anaesthetic and a link to who she was when she was whole and someone's wife. But with the peeling open of both eyelids came the sinking feeling as reality attacked her and she was reminded that her husband had left her and her world was no longer a vanilla milkshake life but one of muddy water.

Uselessly, she kept reminding herself that millions of people broke up and it was an everyday occurrence, not a life-threatening one. And then it broke her a little more to think that she lived in a world where a heart breaking was an everyday occurrence and not one where the world should stop still.

Since he left, Alex had not sent her one text, email or even phoned. Sophie had sent him countless; begging, fury, placating, nonchalant. The silence fed a monster inside of her; a kind of wild and foreign grief that she was drowning in. She feared what it was doing to her physically and neuro-logically. Mostly, she was terrified she was going to die of a broken heart.

CHAPTER EIGHT

The nightmare struck again. Sharply sitting up in bed, she searched for Alex until she remembered that he was no longer there. For what felt like the millionth time in less than a week, she checked her phone in case he has called but that provides no results.

Sophie looked around the room and found nothing to comfort her, the gloom seeped through the windows and rolled across the floorboards, where there should be sunlight.

Bile kept rushing to the back of her throat as she swallowed whilst her face was hot and tender from crying. With the television still murmuring in the background, she sat up in bed and pressed her back against the cool stone wall. Which, strangely, soothed her as her heart felt in physical pain, wincing and writhing with each fresh batch of thoughts. It was as if someone had ripped a Band-dAid off mighty fast and left an open wound that wasn't ready to be healed.

Sophie started a silent, movementless cry but was quickly interrupted as a bird flew into the window with a disturbing thud. The sound was enough to shake her out of her misery.

Looking bedraggled in her pyjamas, Sophie cautiously stepped out into her backyard and noticed the small, shiny bird that flew into her window. It lay motionless on the ground. She tiptoed up to it and looked at it for a beat. Unexpectedly, and making Sophie jump, the bird recovered from its shock, shook itself off and flew away.

As she turned back to go inside the house, clutching the loose waistband of her pyjama pants, she notices that there is a thin wire of copper where the bird landed. Too sad to care, she walked back inside whispering to herself, 'I'm falling apart without you, Alex.'

CHAPTER NINE

Sophie shuddered in the waiting room of the doctor's surgery that she'd reluctantly hauled herself to. It wasn't that it was cold, in fact, she felt like a roast chicken inside an oven. But something inside her had stirred up a chill.

The doctor was middle-aged podgy man that didn't really want to be dealing with Sophie and her imaginary problems. At the other side of the desk, he typed without meeting her eyes. 'And has there been any stressful events that have occurred recently?' He asked.

'Well... yeah. My husband left me.'

Nonchalantly nodding, he said 'it's certainly an unusual set of symptoms... the hair loss, the nightmares, sensitivity of taste, smell and touch, sore gums... You say your body hurts?'

Sophie wasn't sure whether it was a question or accusation. 'My whole body feels like a bruise. It's all been happening since just before my thirtieth birthday.

'Hmm. I see. Like I said, it's an unusual set of symptoms but nothing that we can't attribute to stress. Particularly seeing as though your husband left.'

'So what should I do?'

'Take a multivitamin and get as much sleep as you can. Try to get back to your normal routine and structure. I find that always helps when people get a bit... wobbly.'

Sophie looked at him blankly for a bit. 'Do people die from a broken heart?' She murmured.

The doctor stopped what he was doing and turns to face her. 'I'll prescribe you something to help you sleep. You might want to look into finding a good therapist.'

Sophie stood to leave, but hesitated and was about to say something. In the end, she decided against it and walked out.

CHAPTER TEN

Despite the tiredness dragging at her face, Sophie decided to go back to work, welcoming the distraction. Almost looking forward to going back to work and being in a familiar enough environment, she was sure that it would take her away from her cave of misery.

Hurriedly she slipped into her corporate work outfit. Looking in the mirror, she approved of her outfit but was dismayed at her hair and face. She tried to plump up her hair and seeing it fall greasy and limp, settled on tying it back in a sleek ponytail. To herself in the mirror, she announces 'you've got this. This is the kind of normalcy that you need to get better. You don't want Alex to come back and see that you've totally fallen apart, right?' Swiping on a lipstick that made her feel garish rather than put together, she smacked her lips together anyway. 'Good. That'll fool anyone.'

Since Alex left, Sophie told herself that it was near impossible to resign without an income. Until her beloved paintings started to sell, she was tethered to her job. She'd squandered all her sick leave, pining over the Alex-shaped hole in her life.

Usually, she loved being positioned on display at the front of Roman & Associates at the sleek mirrored desk that stood on thin trestle legs and exposed her knees. The desk bore no more than a phone headset and a laptop, she rarely even had the requirement for a pen. People would walk by during their ordinary day and peer in, mostly absentmindedly, but some people who walked the same route regularly made it habit. Often, people would smile or nod. She felt so comfortable being on the fringe of activity, amongst the people but nowhere near being amid people.

But since she'd turned thirty, she struggled to find that same sense of ease. The smiles still came but she found them annoying, rather than pleasant. It was a hassle to smile back and she'd taken to pretending not to see anyone, busy typing up emails and checking the weather on her laptop. What once made her feel attended to, now made her feel uneasy, like a pending disaster was about to occur. Imagined scenarios of trucks losing control and crashing through the two-storey high glass walls or an unnoticed gas leak to spread throughout the building shattered through her mind. She didn't hate her job— although she would prefer to be at home painting— but it was laborious to turn up and use all her spent energy pretending that she wasn't constantly on edge. Sometimes, she felt like a wrongly hanged woman on display in the town square.

Sophie smiled tightly at her colleagues as she slid herself behind the desk, affirming that yes she did, in fact, feel better and it was just a little virus, nothing to be concerned about. They didn't need to know that her husband had left her. Especially when Sophie was sure she would find a way for him to come back.

The morning flew by, just as she had anticipated and was grateful for. She was right, work was just the tonic that she needed. She even had a new idea for a painting she could start working on that night and she was itching to get home to start it.

Around lunchtime, though, things took a turn. After a flurry of couriers had come and gone, a squat woman traipsed in. Initially, Sophie didn't bother looking up until she could see her torso pressed against the desk in front of her. When she lifted her eyesight and saw her face, she ejected herself backwards with her hands, rolling her chair until it hit the wall behind her. The woman donned timeless clown makeup: a powder white face, exaggerated lips and eyes rimmed in black eyeliner, forming pointy triangles halfway down her cheek. She had stripy stockings that sat under satin frilly bloomers and a matching top, frills flopping on her arms as she breathed heavily.

'Sorry, you gave me a fright. How can I help you today?' Sophie quickly tried to refasten her composure.

In response, the woman placed her hands on the desk and leaned as close as she could towards Sophie. 'Durrr dunt dunt duddit derr derr duddit...' The woman moved her head and torso around in a circle whilst humming the *Entry of the Gladiators* circus theme music. Sophie surveyed her as she moved slowly and stared straight ahead, the humming as unnerving as the outfit and movement. Despite herself, Sophie squealed. More out of confusion than straight fear.

A handful of eager colleagues rushed from their hidden offices to attend to Sophie's screams and she turned back to them, fielding away tears that were coming thick and fast. 'What's wrong? What is it?' Came a chorus of concerns.

Sophie pointed and turned back to the clown woman but there was no one there. Just an empty tiled foyer with one strip of sunshine lying across the floor like it belonged there. 'There was a scary woman here! She was just here. I...'

'I didn't see anyone when I came out. Are you okay?'

'She was humming at me! I swear she was right here.' Sophie's hand flapped uncontrollably around her.

Each of her coworkers looked to one another, unsure what to do. Her manager strode out and looked at her compassionately. 'Soph sometimes viruses can take a lot longer to heal than we think. I'm really happy for you to take the rest of the day off with pay. Have a rest and come back tomorrow, if you feel better.'

Sophie didn't bother responding, she knew they thought she was crazy. And they were probably sick of her declining behaviour lately anyway. She hadn't exactly been warm and friendly to everyone. Maybe they had cottoned on that Alex had left her?

Grabbing her handbag, she swept out the front door looking up and down the street to make sure it was clear of any clowns before she went home. There was not a clown in sight.

By the time she'd driven to their white stucco suburban house, she had shaken the nonsense out of her brain. It could have easily been a vagrant off the streets or an actor trying out a bit on her. It really wasn't that big of a deal. But the way she overreacted concerned her. No, it annoyed her. And she felt humiliated and so very exhausted.

Stepping out of the car, she scanned the driveway and the perimeter of her house for any signs of Alex. There were none. But Sophie noticed a small lump at her door. Yet another dead bird and she swiped it away with her foot, disgusted.

Despite being the pointy middle of the afternoon, Sophie crawled into bed, making sure all her doors and windows were locked. Exhaling with enough force to make a dent in the doona, she turned her morning alarm off because she knew that she wasn't going back into work the next day. Or ever again.

CHAPTER
ELEVEN

The storm of humiliation faced her when she awoke the next day. Fearing what her coworkers must think of her, she knew she had no other option but to cut that part of her life off. Close it down, especially so she could focus on healing herself and finding Alex.

Gathering her work suit, she bundled it up and shoved it in a garbage bag, which she stuffed straight into the outside bin.

Opting instead for saggy leggings and a faded turtle neck, she plopped herself on a stool in front of her easel. She liked to draw back the curtains when painting. The wide windows that she sat in front of offered her generous light and a reprieve for her eyes and brain when she needed a rest from staring at the small woven squares of the canvas. Her painting area was the sunniest and brightest spot in the house. But she was careful not to fall into its trap of false optimism, the warmth of the sun liked to trick you into thinking that everything was going to be okay.

Grabbing a jar of brushes, she swirled one around, tapped it on the side and held it under her chin as she contemplated the empty canvas. Her brow furrowed and her face became tense as she navigated her unruly artist's block.

Sophie tried to paint away some of the darkness that had been plaguing her. All whilst skirting around the real things that got to her: Alex leaving, the rock from her nightmares, the clown lady... and tried to paint her feelings manifest. There was a convincing sense of whirling in her head, of settled mud been shaken up in a glass of water. So, she painted a bottle of muddy water, sitting atop a featureless person's head. It left her unsatisfied, so she tipped the canvas off her easel and discarded it on the floor. With a fresh canvas awaiting her, she sighed and looked across her front yard trying to squeeze a commercially palatable image to mind that she could paint, something that would look good in a modern Hampton's style or minimalist style home. Although it bored her, the less evocative it was, the better, for mainstream production. She needed to make some money, somehow.

Through the window, she contemplates her garden. There's a painful stabbing realisation that she would need to attend to it sooner rather than later and that she wouldn't have Alex by her side to pull out the weeds with. In between the plump geranium bushes that line the front fence, something catches her eye. A shiny, white van with dark tinted windows sits directly opposite and Sophie swears she sees a flash of light coming from inside. With held breath, she watches it and waits. Remembering her overactive imagination from the clown incident, she rolls her eyes at herself and captures her loose hair back in a hairband so she can go back to concentrating on painting.

But a figure, dressed mainly in black and khaki, sweeps tactfully from her neighbours' bushes, that border her driveaway, to the opposite side of the road. So swiftly, in not much more time than it took her to blink, the person had alighted the cabin of the van. Sophie didn't catch their face, only a black plain cap. Unsure what to do, she ran to her bedroom where she'd left her phone and pressed open the camera function, only to discover that the van had completely gone by the time she'd reached her front step. This time, unlike the clown, she was sure she hadn't imagined it at all. Although she did convince herself to look for an innocent explanation, to stop seeking the sinister, still very much haunted by the embarrassment of her reaction at work. There was no real reason that anyone should want to harm her or her neighbours. She lived in a middle class, safe suburb and even break-ins were notoriously rare in the area.

Stepping back from the window and abandoning her painting, Sophie Googled 'increasing jumpiness' and self-diagnosed some anxiety. It was true, her increasing hypervigilance came with, or fuelled, her anxiety. There was no question. She glossed over the words 'active stress response', which made complete sense, since Alex leaving was an incredible stressor on her. One that she felt utterly out of control with.

Sophie sighed with despair and finally plucked up enough courage to phone Bree. Sophie clears her throat as it went to voicemail. 'Hey, Bree. It's Sophie. I know we haven't spoken in a bit but I...' Sophie faltered a little. She had no idea what to say or what she wanted from Bree. 'I... can you call me back when you can? Thanks, bye.'

'It's just a bit of cortisol,' she told irritably herself as she rummaged through her cupboards for some camomile tea bags. 'Seriously Sophie, you need to relax. You are making yourself insane.'

With an afternoon yawning before her and a fire inside of her, she scooped her hair up on top of her head and filled a fresh jar with water, thrusting her paintbrushes into it. Sipping at her camomile tea, she focussed her mind on her painting in the hopes it would still her and distract her from her jitteriness. Mindlessly, she squeezed blue, teal, white and grass green worms of paint onto her palette. The strokes came swiftly, deftly and fluidly. The thick streaks of paint seemed to swirl and float back in one itself and made her dizzy. This happened sometimes, she got so focussed on painting that she forgot to eat or hydrate and she'd get dizzy and experience mini hallucinations. She expected this happened to everyone who experienced intense closeness to their work. 'It's no different to people getting swirls in front of their eyes when they stare at a computer screen all day,' she told Alex once. Who just looked at her like she was lying.

Sophie dropped the paintbrush she was holding when a solid thunk hit the window above her. She looked to her toes, a cobalt splatter marring the cool white tiles. She took her shirt off and used it to wipe up the paint, tense that it had stained. If he were there, Alex would have chastised her for it, further adding to his narrative that she was a careless and reckless artist.

'Grrrr. For fuck's sake! Those stupid birds need to realise there's a window there,' she said to no one in particular.

Below the window, outside, lay a ball of a blackbird, its head tucked towards its torso. The bird's feathers had fluffed up, to cover its motionlessness. *Alex can deal with it when he returns home,* she thought. She couldn't be bothered discarding yet another dead bird.

But, like last time she went to inspect a fallen bird, she noticed something beside it. A thin, creamy matchbook lay next to the bird's slackened beak. Admiring the ornate design on the cover, she picked it up and then pocketed it.

CHAPTER TWELVE

'**F**ly.'

A disembodied command woke her up. The air around her yellow and thick. It was afternoon and she had nodded off after leaving her painting half done. The unfinishedness of it replicating how undone her mind and life felt. Her thick slumber was helped by the painkillers she had unearthed at the back of the fridge, leftover from when Alex once had dental surgery. She didn't care whether they would make her more miserable, as long as she got snatches of sleep where she could. A nervous energy had been bound to her, swirling her around the house each day, pushing her to half complete simple tasks. A half-emptied dishwasher, empty toilet rolls spilled through the bathroom, three separate grocery lists had begun and were dotted around the house. The couch housed baskets and baskets of laundry that she felt too heavy to put away, sometimes too tired to even push off the couch, so she just laid on top of. The mail piled up in the letterbox and she had no intention of changing that. His mail was still coming, letters addressed to them, with both their names printed boldly across the front like they were still a family. Which they were most definitely not. It made her sick to think of his current address. Where was he? Who was he with? And the recognisable wash of anxiety scraped through her. Annoyed that the voice demanding that she fly had poked through her rare bit of rest, she rolled over, wanting to slip back into the chocolatey sleep. The TV stared silently and dully back at her, waiting for her to alight it with their familiar routine. She reached her foot towards the curtain, trying to hook it with her toe and push it back, wondering if the voice came from someone outside. Was he back?

Sophie leapt out of bed hoping that he had used his key but she didn't even need to look in the kitchen or lounge room to know he wasn't home. The air was still with loneliness. That icky still feeling when you know that no one has entered the room in a while.

Sighing with despair, she shuffled around the house wearing nothing but greying socks and a faded blue t-shirt, looking from window to window to window, hoping to see anything... but really hoping that her will would be strong enough to bring him to her.

A tiny sparrow collided into the window she stood facing, reverberating as she jumped her socked feet together as if by pressing her legs together she could stop the impact. Outside the window, the clump of bird lay still, folded in on itself. The fluffy plumage stood up in spikes and it could have been mistaken for a baby hedgehog. Sophie left the dead bird— yet another— on the ground as a symbol of all that was dying, was dead, within her.

Suddenly it hit her. The birds, the voice telling her to fly, the pent up angst inside of her. In somewhat of a trance, she knew what she had to do. Sophie flung open her wardrobe and wriggled into a cobalt blue dress and shiny heels.

The tinny beats exploded and made the rest of her body reverberate as she pressed her earbuds firmly into her ears. With each vibration, she felt like she was shaking off a demon, one that followed her everywhere. That demon was the wincing, squeezing pain of anxiety: a twisted stomach, chilled blood and broiling cheeks. The music and the rapid pacing helped to blast away some of the noise that sat in her head and she didn't have to hear her own breathing. The chaos of strangers and her first real foray into this urban wilderness—aside from going to work— provided an unexpected comfort. She timed each beat with a footstep to shake off the chills that the sunshine couldn't touch. But the more she walked, the more she became alert to something uncanny. There was something building inside of her. It felt like sagacity. It pushed aside any need to know where Alex was and why he left. Or why she couldn't get a handle on her nightmares. It was bigger than that. And suddenly, it started to make sense. Slapping her palm to her forehead, she admonished herself for being so daft and resisting a knowledge that was there all along. Her eyes scanned the open-air mall, darting from shop to shop, building to building. Which was the right one? They all looked similar, not fit for her purpose. But there was one, at the mouth of the mall. One that she'd looked at many, many times before. In the past, it was nothing more than familiarity to her ordinary, everyday scene. An invisible prop on a set. But today, this building was something different to her. It was a catalyst. Again, she was embarrassed that something so obvious had been sitting in her mind and she hadn't bothered to listen. Too busy being obsessed over Alex's whereabouts to understand what had been flourishing inside of her this whole time.

A soft mist started to fall, despite the crisp sunshine still out. She felt it hit her skin but didn't feel its dampness or coolness. Her skin was aflame with purpose when her eyes travelled upwards to her chosen building. She remembered visiting the rooftop bar many times, years ago. The fake plants held in concrete planters lining the balcony desecrated with countless cigarette butts. The Friday evenings she would visit would be awash with mid-tier corporate dickheads, with tight suit pants, pointy brown brogues and shirts all the shades of a bruise: lilac, blue and violet.

As she travelled up the clunking, smelly elevator she felt elated at the possibilities of who she was becoming. Or, rather, who she'd missed that she'd been all along. The elevator doors pulled open and presented her with the empty bar and the wide balcony. A bartender had his back to her as he contemplated the rows and rows of bottles lining glass shelves and one bored waiter slowly laid out one knife at a time on the perfectly set tables. The balcony doors were open, despite the threat of the sunshower and the white curtains billowed inwards, an invitation from the angels.

Sophie stepped out onto the balcony, alone, as the curtains whipped around her like she was in a music video. She placed her handbag underneath one of the curtains' hem and stepped towards the balcony rail. The planters were still there, possibly would always be there and she lifted herself onto one, balancing on the thick edge on the balls of her feet. Once she felt the slight rain, only then did she truly feel it— every single sprinkle that touched her skin. She didn't even know that you could feel so much sensation at one time, yet distinguish every tiny pinprick. Her hair whipped back behind her and her navy dress tightened around her thighs as if they were thick horse reins being pulled on. Sophie leant her torso forward and was relieved that she had finally learnt something so obvious. Yanking her earbuds from her ears, she took the fullest breath she felt she ever had and look upwards. She could fly.

'Ahh no, you don't.' A firm but jovial voice commanded her from behind. Sophie felt her dress pull tight against her as someone grabbed hold of it and pulled. She pushed one hand into the railing and leveraged it to turn around and see who was tugging at it. Lemon juice and musk hit her nostrils as a rigid arm shot around her waist and pulled her backwards, a shoe falling off to the side of the planter box. Instinctively, Sophie sucked in her stomach and she felt another arm snake around her, clamping her in between them. Her earbuds toggled around her neck, jostling together.

'I got you. You don't want to do that.' Her skin had lost its tingle and her tongue had lost its words. Confused, she looked at where her shoe had fallen and the clamping arms awkwardly shuttled her towards the otherwise of billowing curtains, where an empty Chesterfield lounge awaited her.

Blink, she told herself. *You must remember to blink. Otherwise, they will suspect something.* All her efforts were focused on trying to blink naturally, normally. But it felt like she was relearning to blink again.

'What's your name?' The arms released from her waist and a man with blonde curls appeared in front of her face. She noticed his hand was clamped down firmly on her forearms, though.

Blink.

He cocked his head and Sophie could see he almost

wanted to smile at her.

Blink.

'Come over there to the bar with me? I need someone to try my new cocktail.' He pointed to the mar-
ble bar with his chin.

'Soph... ie.' *Blink*. Her words were soft and she
yearned for the startling lucidity that she just had.
He nodded like her name was no surprise. Now
that the electrifying clarity had left her, Sophie's
shoulders hunched forward, her chest collapsing
with despair. She looked down to her lap, then her
feet; one shoe on, one foot bare. Her heart ached
for that fleeting invigoration to come back and her
mind flashed to the absence of her husband.

'Come and have a drink, yeah?' His hands slid to
cup the underside of her forearms and he lifted
her and she felt weightless, like the curtains that
still danced behind her. The waitress sidled up to
them and presented her shoe as if she were Cinderella. 'Here you go!' she said proudly, tugging at her
waistcoat with one hand. Sophie didn't say anything but did let her place the shoe in front of her
foot, whilst the bartender didn't break his grip on
her arms. She slid into her shoe and followed him
meekly to the barstool he pointed towards.

Gratefully, she sucked up the syrupy orange drink
he unhurriedly prepared for her. Three sips were
all it took before she was crushed under the weight
of her dismay. Her eyes prickled and filled with
tears. 'What do I owe you?' Sophie asked politely
after she moved the third drink towards her crest-

fallen chest.

'Absolutely nothing. Pull out your phone.'

Sophie shook her head, fearing he was going to ask her out.

'Just do it. I want you to call a friend in front of me to come pick you up.'

The relief of avoiding being asked out made her willingly call Bree to come collect her.

Bree answered almost immediately. 'Soph! So sorry that I have missed your calls. It's late… everything okay?'

'Yeah. No. Hey listen, I know it's an inconvenience but is there any chance you can come pick me up?'

'Where are you?'

'Err… Hotel…' Sophie looked around her as the bartender mouthed the hotel's name at her. '…Richton.'

'I'm not far away. Be there in a few minutes.'

CHAPTER
THIRTEEN

'Have you ever been to therapy before Sophie?' Carla was just the right shrink for her and Sophie was captivated by her from the very first moment. Bree had picked her up, no questions asked and as she dropped her home she pressed the therapist's card into her hand urgently and simply told her, 'it's time.' Sophie was awash with awkward vulnerability telling Bree about the balcony incident but knew in her heart that Bree was right.

The lemony clean voice of the therapist made her feel terrified and safe at the same time and she wanted to give herself all over to her, tell her everything, spread out her hands and vomit in to them. Carla made you feel like if you could just place it all in her hands, if only for a moment, she would wash your soul sterile by taking your cares and throwing them off a cliff.

Sophie contemplated holding back on her answer. But knew that she'd only be cheating herself. 'Once. When I was five.'

'Oh?'

Sophie's eyes travelled around the room and then land on Carla. Sophie reasoned that she might as well jump in. 'Well, I don't want us to get derailed by this information because it's not really why I'm here. But when I was five, both my parents were killed in a car accident. I had a few sessions with a child psychologist, of which I cannot remember much about. I remember he had a bright orange fluffy puppet with angry eyebrows that sat lifeless in the corner, though. But that's it. Ruth, my guardian, said I had threatened to run away if she made me go to any more sessions. And since I was a fairly compliant child, she didn't see the need for me to keep going.'

'It sounds like you were great at setting your boundaries from an early age. That is something to be proud of.'

Sophie had never considered that. Instead, admonishing herself for being petulant her whole life.

'Anyway, I hear that you're not here to talk about the death of your parents, which we can always revisit by the way. Now, are you affiliated with any particular belief systems or religion? These are quite fundamental questions when you start therapy. It's just so I can get to know you.'

'No, never been interested or even that exposed to

religion, to be honest.' A flicker of what could have been disapproval went through Carla. Sophie knew it was her imagination kicking up again though. She'd been honing in and seeking out any kind of rejection that she could find from Carla, however subconscious. At the first flicker of rejection, Sophie knew she'd have an out and wouldn't have to return to confront the ugly and terrifying parts of herself.

'So why are you here, Sophie?'

Sophie presses her lips together to stop from crying. 'My husband. He's left. And I... am... distressed.'

Something flashes across Carla's face that is indistinguishable to Sophie. 'Were you happy in the marriage?'

'Yes!' Sophie declared, defensively.

'Do you remember first meeting him?'

'Of course. I took notice of him the very first second I saw him. It was back when I lived at Ruth's...'

Sophie thought back to when she met Alex. After her parents died, her mother's cousin, Ruth, took her in. Which was more of a formality than an actuality as Ruth had a tendency to live in a world where fairies existed far more than responsibilities did.

Ruth had bright orange hair, dyed from a box which she had stocked up on; three full shelves of it in the cupboard. She demanded Sophie brush on the garish dye so she could continue smoking and watching her awful melodramas on TV. Within a month, an inch of white hair would protrude from her scalp and she'd croak at Sophie that it was time to do her hair again, even if it was late on a school night. Which she didn't mind because she wasn't that interested in school anyway. The other kids called her Ghost Girl, which was predominantly for the way she looked with her translucent hair and skin. But Sophie always felt it because she felt exactly like a ghost: invisible and floating around unnoticed. To others, the innocence that her face portrayed was alarming and almost off-putting. As if it brought into question your own lesser existence. If you could bear long enough to stare at her without questioning yourself, you would probably notice a mild superhuman quality. Sophie's movements always seemed gently calculated. The fairylike whisper of the way she brushed her palms together, reaching an angelic arm behind her neck to gather a handful of hair to sweep to the opposite shoulder, the constant need for her feet to be near one another and the long lines of her legs that followed. Ladylike, gentile, graceful... words that applied but were also rejected with disdain for they meant something that she felt she was not.

Ruth was partial to expensive pastel coloured kaftans that featured peacocks and sequins and her knobbly fingers were decorated in thick gold rings, even though she barely left the house. She spoke of no lover and no friends so it shocked Sophie to hear that she had absconded with a rich man to Greece, not long after Sophie moved out at age twenty.

'I've called someone. They're on their way,' Ruth said as Sophie swiped more copper hair dye on her head.

'What do you mean?'

'Someone to install cameras. I'm sick to death of being watched.'

'Who is watching you?'

'Out there!' Ruth pointed to the backyard with her cigarette balancing between her fingers, which were thinner than the cigarette's body. 'In the bushes and whatnot. Someone has got their eye on me and I'm sick of it. Sneaking around through the bushes, spying on me. I'm in no mood to have a peeping tom.'

'I haven't seen anyone out there.'

'No, well that's because you haven't been paying attention.'

'Do you think maybe you're thinking of one of your shows you've been watching? Didn't that happen to one of the characters the other day?'

'If I say there's some creeper out there, then there is.'

There was a knock at the door.

'Anyway, now I can prove it because those guys are here to install some security cameras. Let them in,' Ruth barked at Sophie, not leaving the safety of her velvet recliner.

Ruth was not terribly unkind but she was neg-lectful in a way that left Sophie feeling constantly invisible, so when Alex walked into her house, in all his luminous youth, in his thick work boots and navy coveralls, holding a reel of cabling in one hand and a takeaway coffee in the other, and looked at her like he'd recently gained the gift of sight, Sophie felt like she existed for the very first time.

The security cameras were installed, taking a lot longer than other clients', and Alex would hold Sophie's gaze for a little longer than she could stand, throughout the day. She was shocked that Alex could even see her.

On the final day of installation, Alex walked in holding two coffees: one for himself and one for Sophie, which she gratefully accepted.

A few months later, Sophie moved out of Ruth's smoked-filled house and into a small one bed-roomer with Alex, where they began their romantic bliss. They had barely been apart since. What's more, is they rarely argued in the decade they had been together. A bit of spirited bickering that forced them to roll their eyes at each but nothing serious. Except for that one tepid afternoon. Still, Sophie didn't think it had anything to do with much, really.

They had been lounging in the backyard, Alex had spread a tartan blanket on the grass for them to lay on. Sophie lay, her arm shielding the sun from her eyes and her pallid sticklike legs getting washed in warmth. It was the kind of gently warm day that made them both feel the promise of summer, although still far away. Alex handed her a glass of icy wine and they sipped it amongst the provocative floral waft of the afternoon. Sophie rested her head on his thigh, not even flinching when the condensation dropped onto her forehead from Alex's wine glass. There was perfection in the moment. The only flaw was the neighbour's noisy lawnmower, chewing and grinding from one side of their yard to the other.

But, as always, it was merely another calm before a storm.

Alex wiped away a condensation drop from her cheek with his thumb. 'Do you think if your parents hadn't ended their lives that they would like me?' He asked hopefully.

Sophie's body stiffened and she looked at his eyes, which were earnestly shining back at her. Her torso shot upright and she spilled her wine on the rug.

'Careful!' He warned her but was laughing as he shook the puddle off onto the grass. 'I'll get you another.' He stood up. But Sophie stood up just as quickly and watched his chambray shirted back disappear into the house. It wasn't long before he ducked back out with a full wine glass, almost comically to the brim.

Sophie stood where she was, not moving.

'Is the blanket too wet? I'll get a towel.' He said as he graciously handed her the wine which she refused to take.

'How dare you,' Sophie whispered.

'What's that, my love?'

'I said, how dare you.'

'How dare I what?'

'You said my parents took their own lives. They were in a car accident, Alex! Is that what you think? That they did it on purpose?'

'Oh, baby.' He reached out to draw her in his arms but she remained frozen on the spot, watching the wine tip over the lip of the glass. 'When did I say that?'

'Just then! You asked me if they would like you if they didn't end their lives!'

'Oh sweetie, no! I said "if their lives hadn't of ended", he looked shocked and his face went a peculiar shade of grey. He searched the ground for somewhere to put the glasses. 'You must have misheard me.'

'I didn't mishear you. I know what I heard.'

'I didn't say what you think I said, Sophie,' Alex's voice became serious. 'Why don't you finish your wine and we can enjoy the warmth a little longer? Maybe have a nap if you like?'

She took the wine from his hand and gulped it as she marched back into the house and ran a bath, so she could get away from Alex be alone with her thoughts. She was certain that's what he said. But as she finished her wine and soaked in the rose-scented foam, she became less and less certain. She must have misheard him.

Sophie brought herself back to the therapist's room and regaled an edited version of how they met. 'We've been so happy together ever since.

Well, til now. And here I am,' she splayed her hands out in front of her.

'And I'm glad you're here. Please, have some more tea,' Carla offered.

CHAPTER
FOURTEEN

The cool afternoon after her first therapy session disappointed her. Instead of feeling better, Sophie felt undone. Her thoughts were playing a coarse game of sport and she could barely spot the ball from her vantage point. It wearied her but not enough to stop the rampant inner tornado of self-blame. Her mind retraced over and over, the things she said. How did she come across? What did she say? Did she even believe some of the things she said? Knowing that as well as failing her first therapy session, she also failed the aftermath.

Audibly, she groaned to her empty house. She could not stand her own mental swirl so she slid to the kitchen, opening the bottom drawer and pressed out two tiny white tablets from their crackling tray. She bit it and swallowed the two halves, the acrid taste forcing her to wince. Some-where, at the back of her mind, she remembered reading that biting them made them work faster. To be sure, she held the second tablet underneath her tongue willing it to absorb into her blood-stream from her gums, rather than the painfully long and drawn out digestive process, until she could no longer stand the taste.

'Aark. Aark.' The crow, in the tree outside her back door, shouted at her so she flung the door back, stepped out underneath it and looked at it in the eye.

'Why don't you just shut the hell up?' she said mali-ciously. It looked at her with disdain, its chocolate eye rolling over her. And then it lazily flew off, as if shrugging her away.

Back in her bedroom, she rearranged the pillows around her in bed so that when the nightmare came, she would be safely cocooned from herself.

CHAPTER FIFTEEN

A few days later, Sophie sat across from her therapist, for what seemed like both the second and the hundredth time. She surprised herself by not giving up on therapy. There was a pull in Sophie that was greater than her pain. Waiting for Carla's prompts, she pulled away her light scarf. Although too hot in the room, especially with the warm herbal tea Carla offered, it was a source of comfort and made Sophie feel like she was being held. How much she wanted to demand that a window be opened for once, the stench of a thousand people's breath stuck on the walls and furnishings. But Sophie was determined to be a good, polite girl.

Carla positioned herself neatly in a grey linen chair, in a professional outfit that was neither fashionable nor comfortable. The ensemble was deliberately chosen to incite approachability and assuredness. But that did not stop Sophie from spending a lot of time looking at her therapist's feet; beige stockinged feet in a square-toed heel underneath navy pants. She reminded Sophie of a more serious version of Elaine from Seinfeld.

Sophie was desperate to keep building trust with and please Carla, not only for her own progress but because she couldn't escape the fear that Carla would get bored of her soon enough and palm her off to a colleague. Especially once she realised she was beyond being helped. Like most, Sophie grabbled with the notion that there was something fundamentally wrong with her and no one in this lifetime could fix her. Alex leaving her had done nothing but confirmed this truth.

Carla watched Sophie with umber coloured eyes behind her wireframe glasses. 'What are you thinking about right now, Sophie?'

'This morning, there was another dead bird outside my window. Although I didn't kill it, I feel responsible.'

Carla seemed pleased by this answer and scribbled at her notes, tapping the top of her pen on the notepad resting on her lap in approval. There was a small pile of birds waiting for Sophie at home. It looked like a pile in a toy shop. They kept flying to their death against the window, despite Sophie stringing up some unused Christmas bunting.

'In what way?'

'I don't know really. Shouldn't I be able to save it?'

'It's not uncommon to feel the burden of a saviour complex when we are unable to essentially save ourselves,' she said sensibly.

Sophie didn't know why she said what she said next. Perhaps she was desperate to shock Carla out of their power dynamics. Perhaps it was she who was bored. 'Birds say things to me.'

Carla twitched almost unnoticeably. 'Do you often think that birds can talk to you?'

Sophie could feel her goading her but decided to press on anyway. 'The birds communicate with me. In a way. Which is exactly what a crazy person would say, I know. Anthropomorphism is one of the most prominent delusions.' Sophie didn't give Carla time to confirm or interject. 'It's not like a bird will come to me and start speaking in English but more that their behaviour is noticeable. Hard to ignore. There are cascades of warbles at irregular times in the night. Often, I wake up believing it's morning but it's still the same day that I fell asleep. They trill at my window and I have no idea what they are really saying but I do trust that they are talking to me. I absorb their sounds and wait for translation that often appears as my own thought-forms or epiphanies within the proceeding days,' Sophie let the words tumble out. Only after they had left her mouth did she feel the indignity of revealing too much.

Carla sensed her hesitation. 'Go on,' she prompted by rolling her hand and pen.

'Sometimes, like when my mind is a bit clearer,

I try to concentrate really hard to translate what they're telling me. I can barely explain but I just know they have deliberately chosen me to talk to. I just don't know why.'

Sophie stopped looking at Carla's shoes and watched her face and waited. But Carla surprised her by encouraging her.

'You know Sophie, I can see why you would say that birds are communicating with you.'

Sophie let out a big breath of air. Carla showed no trace that she was terrified of Sophie or that she was going to have her sanctioned.

Carla pointedly looked at the clock and nodded at her. 'I'd like to hear more about this. I'm afraid our time is up for today. If it's alright with you, let's continue this conversation in our next session? We can schedule it earlier if you'd like.'

Sophie was perplexed, unsure where the time had gone but shook her head in agreement. *Sure*, she thought to herself, *the damage has already been done*. As she gathered up her things to leave, she glimpsed Carla's scrawled handwritten notes and noticed "birds" had been underlined three times and was ticked.

Surprising herself and Carla, Sophie eagerly came back to therapy the next day, at Carla's insistence. Carla wiggled her bottom into her chair after placing fresh, steaming cups of tea in front of them both.

Sophie fiddled with something in her pocket—the matchbook she found the other day. With a sense of smugness, Sophie felt she had already endured life's tragedies and that the rest of her lifetime was her own. Naively falling into the knowing that all her life's bad had already occurred, she expected the rest of her life to be a comfortable and healthy experience with no unexpected turns. But Alex leaving had upended her sense of self and stability. From her current viewpoint, the rest of her life now seemed extremely shaky. Because she'd never planned on anything going awry, she'd never developed the resilience or mechanisms to cope. Sophie fiddled with something in her pocket as she debated going down yet another rabbit hole.

'No word from Alex still?'

Sophie sadly shook her head.

'Where do you think he is? He must be somewhere, surely?'

'If I knew...' Sophie paused, unsure how to even finish her sentence. 'I don't understand why this has made me fall apart so much. I've been orphaned and still managed to never fall apart, in fact it made me stronger!'

Looking back, she should have been ragingly embarrassed by this state of comfort and foolishness. The very kind of state that almost always preludes disaster. She couldn't help but think it was all her fault that she was incredibly underprepared.

Carla screwed up her face in response and Sophie immediately relaxed into her visible empathy. 'You know, sometimes— particularly as kids— we suppress things that are the most painful to us. Especially if we haven't learnt emotions and how to process them. This incident might actually be triggering dormant pain and grief that you never had the chance to process properly.' Carla paused to sip on her tea and watched Sophie over the rim of her cup.

Sophie didn't want to believe her. Her whole life she had been waiting to "properly" feel the pain of losing her parents. She compared herself to books and movies where people had been left an orphan and had either turned wayward or felt an intense longing. But she couldn't relate at all.

'Let me ask you this. Do you remember much about your parents, particularly right before they died?'

Sophie felt uncomfortable with the question but mainly because there was nothing to retrieve. 'Nothing. It's blank.'

'Good. Good. What's your biggest fear?'

Sophie felt an immediate rage sweep through her body, pooling in her head. What an odd question. *That's just resistance*, she told herself. *This is what therapists do. Most of their job is to push your buttons and then help you work through the reaction.*

'Going insane,' she confessed.

'Interesting.' Carla scribbled down some notes but Sophie could no longer hear the scratching of the pen on the paper as her body seemed to float downwards away from her thoughts and her mouth, which felt stuck in front of Carla.

'And do you feel like you are going insane?' Carla jerked her pen to a stop and lifts only her eyes at

Sophie to extract an answer, who is blankly staring out the window.

'Sophie?' Carla snapped at her.

'Sorry... I... Yes, I feel like I'm going insane.'

'What has been happening to make you think that?

'There's the lack of sleep, the weird things I'm seeing and hearing, my senses are changing... it's like... I don't know what it's like! I've never experienced this before. I mean, I get that people get sad when their husbands leave them out of nowhere. But this? It's like I have a disease. Not to mention the nightmares! And imagining people spying on me in vans? That's just ludicrous.'

Sophie felt deflated and landed back in her body with a thud.

'Our minds tend to tell us about this big scary thing that is going to happen in the future, which never really comes. Meanwhile, the reality is that you are experiencing that very thing— by your own admission— anyway. And my guess is that it doesn't really measure up to how awful your mind is telling you that it's going to be.'

'Well, I wouldn't say it's exactly a dream.'

'Sure. But just to notice how it's nowhere as terrifying as the images the mind is throwing up at you when you contemplate "going insane".'

The way she did air quotations made Sophie mad again, so she tried not to look at her hands and kept taking in streams of air strongly through her nose, to stop herself from lashing out at Carla.

Carla was merely doing her job and Sophie was wise enough to know that she didn't even really understand the therapeutic process and had lost sight of the bigger picture. She trusted Carla to hold up a light into the dark recesses of her untrustworthy mind and guide her out of the obscurity.

'Why do you need to know about my greatest fear?'

'There are two main reasons. Firstly, if I can shine a light of reality on your fear, it can often dissipate. You should see what happens to some people when they let their biggest fear go! I've seen clients book acting gigs, have a family, fly around the world... you get the idea. And secondly, once I know your greatest fear, I can acknowledge it and do everything I can to make you feel as safe as possible. Because in safety, healing can flourish.'

The anger bubbled away and Sophie felt grateful that Carla existed and that she was so willing to help her. It made her want to cry with a pathetic relief.

'What are you experiencing Sophie?'

'Well, lots of emotions, I guess. I'm not sure how to articulate.'

'That's okay. Just say what you can and we can talk about it more over our coming sessions. Do you commit to more sessions, Sophie?'

'Yes. I promise.'

'Good.'

Sophie quickly dismissed the thought that Carla just wanted more money from Sophie. Showing up was the biggest indicator to success with therapy, just like going to the gym. The more time went on, the more she wanted to get better for herself, not just for Alex.

'Before you go, I thought we could try a little hypnosis. Have you undergone any hypnosis?' Carla put her notes and pen to one side and lightly slapped her palms on her knees.

'Not really. Do you think that's the right thing for me though?'

'I believe so, yes. Don't worry, it's not all trances and being unable to control your actions like you see in the movies. It's a very controlled process which is akin to a deep relaxation.'

'You think it would help with the nightmares?'

'I think it would help with the relaxation centres in your brain. Help to activate them more frequently and on command, so that your anxiety and paranoia reduce. As for the nightmares, who's to say? There are plenty of case studies of people who have had success with hypnosis treating their night time worries. But, for you, the best thing we can do is try it for at least three sessions and monitor your nightmare activity closely. Perhaps keep a journal? I'll only be a phone call away, should anything arise for you that we need to address urgently.'

'I guess we could try it. For three sessions you reckon?'

'Yes, and if it seems to be helping you curb your symptoms than we can continue with a few more. Put it this way, you don't have a lot to lose.' Carla placed her hands on top of one another and cocked her head to the side, smiling. She skilfully put Sophie at ease and was right, she didn't have a lot to lose.

'Okay, I'm happy to try it. I'm kinda running out of options.'

'Good. Well, we can start now. I'm a trained clinical hypnotherapist and it's a very simple process. You can either remain sitting or lie down on the couch, if you prefer. It's totally up to you, whatever you are most comfortable with.'

Sophie let her eyelids swoop down, almost relieved to be able to rest, to stop talking, thinking about the next thing she was going to say and what that all meant and how she could put her mind back together. Carla's office was so warm, it was like a hug and Sophie was ready to succumb the second that Carla's slow, dripping voice talked her into the hypnosis process.

Disappointingly, Sophie fell asleep. At least she had hoped she had. Otherwise the hypnosis had worked more powerfully than she ever expected and it was exactly like all those TV shows and magician performances, which she had never believed were real. Surely, they were staged? Humans can't just succumb to the will of another with a few vocal prompts. If they did, then why don't they do weird shit every time they fall asleep in front of the TV or listening to true crime podcasts?

'I'm sorry Sophie, it looks as though it didn't work. I'd be willing to try again next time, if you are? I still think it could be very beneficial, particularly with the nightmares.'

Sophie couldn't help but feel that Carla was incensed with her, even though she delivered her words with softness and delicacy behind a smile. There was something in her eyes and the way Carla's hands had tensed around the ends of the chair arms that led Sophie to believe that whatever she had done, she had failed Carla.

Sophie stepped out of Carla's office in a jumper and thick khaki coat that belonged to Alex. Despite her detest for hats, she wore a beanie— another of Alex's— so she didn't have to smell her unwashed hair and to keep warm, even it was a mild day. She was soon becoming acclimatised to Carla's warm office.

Sophie spotted Bree standing across the street and wiped and blinked her bleary eyes, still sticky from hypnosis. As she rushed over to her, it dawned on her that she missed spending time with her new friend.

'I almost didn't recognise you in your activewear Bree!'

'Hmmm.' Bree didn't look that happy to see her and Sophie wondered if she'd done something wrong. Maybe she overestimated their friendship? Was Bree put off getting too close to her after Sophie told her she heard voices and tried to fly? She could hardly blame her.

'What are you doing in this part of town?' Sophie asked with less enthusiasm.

'Oh, I just thought I'd do some shopping. That gourmet supermarket is meant to have amazing local produce, you know?' Her eyes lit up again and Sophie admonished herself for reading too much into things. She probably had a fight with her husband or had other things on her mind. Sophie found it hard to ignore the stress— or was it a cringe?— in the lines of her eyes.

'I've just been having a therapist's appointment. The one you recommended. Over there.' Sophie pointed across the road and then it hit her. Another cringe-worthy interaction with her new friend. No wonder she didn't want to stop and chat like old pals, she was probably on her way to have her own appointment with Carla and, understandably, didn't want anyone to know about it. 'I must let you go then, I know how busy you are,' Sophie wanted to hug her. The desire to take her hand was paramount. But, learning from her mistakes, she vowed to reign in any awkward behaviour and stop crossing boundaries with Bree. At least until they got to know each other better.

'Oh yes, I must shove on.' Bree stepped forward onto the road without saying goodbye and left Sophie standing there. But before she crossed the road, Bree turned back and said, 'Soph? Look after yourself, okay?'

There was something familiar about the way that Bree regarded her. Something that she couldn't quite place. Throwing herself into her car, Sophie was furious when it hit her. It was the same kind of look that Alex used to give her. And if she thought about it hard enough, it was the same look that was fighting its way through Carla's professional veneer. The condescending bullshit that Bree just served up to her was more than she could bear. Did everyone in the world think she was so fucking crazy that she couldn't take care of herself?

Sophie looked in the car's rearview mirror to try and see what they all saw. Did they see an untameable, yet unbalanced, wildness? Or did they just see a really tired woman that they didn't have the energy to deal with herself? Did they see themselves in Sophie so much that it shocked them? Made them want to run away and not face the shadows inside themselves?

It's true. I'm going mad. Nope, I've already gone mad. Surely, because I've lost a little weight, haven't washed my hair in a little while and the dark circles under my eyes have turned from lilac to slate, that I'm not completely worth abandoning. Is it not uncommon to let yourself go a little when the love of your life leaves you? Is it?

Sophie pushed her face closer towards the car's review mirror, palms pressing into the steering wheel. She waggled her eyebrows and smoothed her hairline away from her forehead. Deep valleys of scar white skin remained where hair used to be. Pulling her hands away from her head she watched as with them came half a dozen strands of hair, lifeless strings that floated down like leaves.

She was going bald at age thirty.

Still stuck on Bree's behaviour as she drove home, Sophie noticed a faceless man driving behind her. At first, she thought— hoped— it was Alex. But it was hard to tell. The reflection of the glary day wiped out his features although she spotted him rubbing a darkened chin with the back of his hand. The rest of his face was erased by his black forward wheeled drive. Sophie didn't like the way his car is leering close to the edge of hers so she sped up, to see what the car would do. After a short moment, the car behind her seemed to speed up too. Which could have been totally instinctual and automatic on the driver's behalf. Especially if they were in a hurry to get somewhere. But there was a gnawing in her gut that convinced otherwise. Instinctively, she shut off the radio to heighten her vigilance. When she ducked down a small residential side street, the sleek black car behind her sharply turned into the same street. That was all the proof Sophie needed.

She quickly rounded a corner into a smaller street lined with cream houses that all bore turrets of rose bushes, bumping her back tyre on the kerb as she missed the angle in her flight. Despite being terrified that someone would unwittingly step out in front of her, she sped up as fast as her sensibilities would allow. But her speed was halted short with a jerk of her foot on the brakes causing an alarming screech. The movement was enough to dislodge the hair from behind her ears and she gasped as the seatbelt squeezed her tight. A dead-end street. There was no one else in the street until two front doors either side of her flung open to investigate out the noise. Carefully and slowly, she made a big effort of turning her car around the cul de sac and headed where she came from, embarrassed to see that no car was following her.

Turning right out of the rose lined cul de sac before anyone would dare yell at her for disturbing their suburban peace, she spotted the dark car waiting, sandwiched in between two parked cars. She had a split second to decide whether to turn left and head back to the main road, pull up beside and confront him or speed past him. None of the options would give her any answers or seem to calm her racing heart down. In a moment of bravery, she shot past and blasted her horn at him. Just so he would know that she knew. 'I can fucking see you,' she said behind the safety of her car windows.

But she was wrong. She couldn't see him because as she blurred past, it wasn't a him at all. It was a woman. Although she couldn't really see into the driver's seat properly, she saw the unmistakable thin face and shoulder length hair of a woman and slim fingers resting on the steering wheel. Flicking her eyes to her mirror, the car didn't bother to follow her any further and Sophie began to feel a wave of humiliation as her heart went back to its regular beats.

Of course, no one was following me. Why on earth would they? A mere coincidence is all. This paranoia is going to kill you Sophie. She chided herself.

CHAPTER SIXTEEN

It wasn't long before Sophie was back ready to empty herself to Carla. An emergency appointment was arranged the next day, at Carla's insistence, after she briefly explained on the phone about her paranoia about the car following her. Even sketching it out loud with her words made her realise how untethered to reality she was. In moments.

Sophie scuffed her shoes across the welcome mat and embraced the pungent incense that clung to her hair the moment she stepped inside the reception room. Her days were empty without Alex but therapy quickly gave her a sense of something that neared purpose.

The therapy room door was open. Carla didn't get up from her chair and called for Sophie from the cave of her office. Her smile was so warm that it pricked Sophie's eyes a little. How could a person that barely knew her, have such softness for her? Even after all her delusions and hallucinations had been revealed. *I guess that's what you do when you're getting paid*, she thought. Which reminded Sophie that she would soon have to work out a way to get an income. Without Alex and her job, she was unsure how the bills would get taken care of.

Carla bent over the low coffee table that sat between them and waved her hand over a mug of urine coloured water which was emitting cylinders of steam. 'I made you a lemon and ginger tea. I know that's your favourite.' Carla gave her a reassuring wink. It certainly was her favourite. Or it was quickly becoming so. The prickly tang, combined with the considerateness of it made just for her, gave her great consolation. She reminded herself to get some teabags so she could replicate the feeling at home.

'Great to see you again Sophie. It's so impressive how you keep showing a commitment to turning up to our sessions. It really does bode well for your success.'

'Yeah.' Sophie wanted to believe her, to trust her completely. And she almost did. But it was hard to shake the tendrils of disbelief off.

'You don't have to answer me now but I would really like you to think about coming more frequently. Four times a week is not uncommon in times of heightened stress.' Carla's hands jiggled beside her.

'Oh. That's certainly something I would have to think about.' Sophie's avoided Carla's eyes by letting them dart around the room, over her streamlined bookshelf, her almost empty desk, the asinine motivational quote on the wall.

'Let's proceed, shall we?'

Sophie recapped what happened in her car and what she had told Carla about the birds at a previous session. She was careful to tell them exactly the same way she had previously and Carla was careful to keep her reaction in check.

'None of this seems particularly out of the ordinary in times of stress,' Carla reassured her. But Sophie couldn't help feeling like Carla was impatient about something or wanted to probe her deeper.

They tried hypnotherapy again with some more success. 'I want you to travel back in your mind's eye Sophie, way back. Back to a time which you think you may not even remember. But you do. Our memories can always be accessed. And you are allowing yourself to access as many memories as you want now, knowing you are safe and they are merely memories.'

Carla paused and Sophie heard her sip some water. At least she was still aware of her surroundings, despite the weight in her legs. It was the most relaxed that Sophie had felt in her body for months.

Carla's pleasant voice dripped all around her. 'Take yourself back to a time when you were very little. Back when your parents will still alive. And tell me, what do you remember? What do you see?'

Sophie shifted in her seat. All of a sudden it was really uncomfortable to be in her body, in that chair that she normally found so comfortable.

'Sophie? What memories are coming up for you?'

Sophie tried to squeeze her mind into a semblance of a memory but nothing seemed to come.

'It's okay, take your time. Breathe,' Carla reassured her.

Pushing aside her own impatience and fear, Sophie could feel a memory arising. She found herself hoping that it would be a vision of her parents.

'Tell me what do you see Sophie?'

'I see... I see...' Sophie humped forward dejectedly. She shot her eyes open in protest. 'This isn't working.'

Carla looked mad. 'It sounds like it did. What did you see Sophie? Was it something upsetting?'

'No, it was just the fucking rock from my nightmares. Honestly, I'm sick of it and it's clearly taking up too much space in my mind and clouding anything important that I store in there.'

'Do you think the rock is in some way connected to your parents' death?' Carla prodded so gently that Sophie almost felt sorry for her, having to baby Sophie in that way. Was she really that petulant or fragile?

'I have considered that in the past but the accident report makes no mention of any rock. The car just flipped, seemingly on its own accord. The report suggested that my dad was driving way too fast on a country road. I'm unsure where exactly. I've never been back to the spot,' Sophie shrugged non-chalantly.

'Hmm. Perhaps the rock represents something to you? A symbol?'

Sophie shrugged again. She'd been through this pop-psychology nonsense with herself before, reading all the dream interpretation books she could find. For a few months, she believed the rock represented her unexpressed grief and she tried to force herself to cry by watching movies where people's loved ones died. Or newspaper articles that bore great tragedy. And although sad, the nightmares did not change course.

'Look, don't force it. With a few more sessions of hypnotherapy, we are bound to figure it out between us.'

Sophie felt somewhat assured. Even if Carla was pretending for both their sake's that Sophie, as a problem, could be fixed, she didn't mind. It was endearing that someone cared enough to try and to listen to her and acknowledge her dreams. Alex, although concerned, always seemed so dismissive when she tried to research her way to the bottom of them. Sometimes, she wondered if perhaps Alex found her more appealing because she had the nightmares. Less of a Ghost Girl and more of a three-dimensional story.

Slam!

A thin man in exaggerated makeup crashed himself up against the window, peering in. His eyes were forced wide open and his lids were painted like peacocks. The sides of his fists were creamy as they pressed against the window and his mouth hung open, his jaw pushed forward. Carla jumped and her blouse followed a split second later. Sophie silently and strangely wished it was a bird against the window so Carla could attest to the strange avian phenomena.

Slam!

He raised and slammed his fists again on the window, despite already having their attention. The few plants behind him rippled with his action. The window faced onto a neglected, unused courtyard that was home to nothing more than some red bricks and some wilting palms. Sophie was unsure how it was even accessed as she only ever came in from the door facing the street and there seemed to be no door leading out to it from Carla's office. Running her eyes around the windowsill, Sophie could see that the window was painted shut, hence the lack of fresh air in the room.

Carla turned back to face Sophie, a hand pressed into her sternum and she let a whistle of air out. 'That made me jump!' she said, almost cheerily. 'Look, can you excuse me? I'll be right back. It's actually a patient of mine. Nothing to worry about. Will not be long.'

By the time Carla was outside mollifying the visibly frustrated man, Sophie had reached across the room to pick up a book that was glaring at her from the shelf. It wasn't planned, to grab the book, but now that it was in her hands she realised that it had been harping at her curiosity every single therapy session since she started. Often counting the books on the shelf— ten— as a nervous habit, as a distraction from the pronounced vulnerability that occurred every time she uncurled in her therapist's office.

The book's cover was brown and looked almost mouldy in certain lights. It was the size of an envelope but held the weight of *The Bible*. A cursory glance suggested it was doused in marketing, or even of some ancient significance. She flipped it over to reveal the front cover. Pressed out in bronze lettering was the title, *Venus*, with no author attribution, in fact, nothing else on the cover except the title. Inside were hand sketches of the planet, with various animals and symbols— some recognisable and ordinary, some not. *How adorably absurd*, Sophie thought to herself. And reached to put the book back. As she tipped the top part of the spine back into the shelf, her sight was caught by the open gape of Carla's handbag. Nestled between an umbrella and some kind of fabric, was an object so familiar that Sophie felt a rush of nausea. Sophie would have recognised the glint anywhere. Instinctively, she bent down to pick it up but snapped her hand back, jolted by the guy outside who started shouting at Carla, his words garbled by the thick glass and the speed at which he was talking. Carla had her hands clasped patronisingly at her chest like she had just announced to a two-year-old that they were going to sing a song. Sophie watched as he leaned his face in closer and drew in a mean breath and she waited for Carla to be struck. But the guy lifted his chin and let his lips fall into a dangling frown and he shuffled away, his arms lifeless.

Carla, with her hands still clasped, turned to the window and looked directly at Sophie. Her eyes darted to her handbag on the floor and back up to Sophie's face with a tender recognition. Quickly, her face squeezed into a large grin.

Sophie quickly sat back down in her well-worn position as Carla stormed back inside, out of breath. She'd been running.

'So sorry about that. He's just a little agitated. I was trying to help him. Medication problems. You gotta feel for him, you know? Now, where were we?' Carla cocked her head, daring Sophie.

'I hope you don't mind, I just had a quick squiz at your books. That brown one is so gorgeous!' Sophie was rushing through her words but had her mind on what was in Carla's handbag.

'Yes, it's a lovely little gift book someone gave me once. Sophie, are you okay? You seem rattled. Did my other patient upset you? I assure you he's fine.' She looked at the ceiling to avoid looking at the bag and to buy time to work out how she could get another look inside. A closer look. Just to be sure that what she had seen was right. 'No, I'm completely okay. I'm sure you've got a handle on it. I was actually forcing myself to remember to grab some of that yummy tea on my way home. Where do you get it?'

'Mmm yes. I can't really remember. I'll have a think and let you know next session, okay? Drink up! You have hardly touched today's cup.'

Sophie mechanically sipped and bluffed her way through the rest of the therapy session but it was obvious to both of them that she couldn't stop thinking about what was in her bag. Keys held by a distinctive copper keyring. Alex's keys.

CHAPTER SEVENTEEN

Once again forgetting to pick up the beloved tea, Sophie scrambled inside her house frantically throwing open the top two kitchen drawers. Swishing aside cutlery and ancient receipts, batteries, bits of homeless plastic, cords and cables. Desperate to see the oval keyring that she was so used to seeing in their house, in Alex's hands, in his pockets, on the kitchen bench where she had to repeatedly toss them out the way. She yanked his bedside drawer out from its home and tipped the contents—an expired nasal spray, three pens, clean tissues, more cords— all over the bed, swiping them aside with her hand. His set of keys weren't there. Exasperated, she kicked the pyramid of clothes in the corner of their bedroom. 'You could have at least had the fucking decency to do your washing before you left Alex,' she shouted at no one. Her toe connected with a clunk of metal. Desperately, she hoped it was his keys. But it was merely the buckle on his best weekend belt and, sadly, the pockets of his jeans turned up especially empty, except for a scrap of paper. Scrutinising the paper, Sophie gasped when she understood what the hand-scrawled address revealed. It was an address she was extremely familiar with. Carla's office!

Why did he have her address written down? Was he a patient too? The temptation to phone Carla and demand to know if Alex was a patient was overwhelming. Of course, she would not be able to tell her for confidentiality reasons. But surely, surely, she would allude to something if she showed enough distress? Was this why Carla had his keys?

Sophie felt her blood cool right down and fall away from her head. The simple explanation of Alex being Carla's patient and having accidentally left his keys in her office was so obvious, now that she was in the sanctuary of her home and had time to recentre herself. Instantly, the panic abated and left Sophie feeling humiliated, even though no one knew what she'd just gone through except herself. Smacking herself in the forehead a couple of times, she said with fury, 'you're a fucking idiot Soph. You need to chill the fuck out a bit once in a while.'

The scattered items across their bed winked at her and she chastised herself even more for her uncontrollable emotions. The panic that was marring her every decision. The mental concoctions that stood in the way of finding real clues to Alex's whereabouts.

The detritus on the bed reminded her that her moods and paranoia were a dysfunction that were severely affecting her life. 'This is exactly why you're seeing a shrink in the first place!' Swiping his drawer contents off the bed and onto the floor, she stalked out to the kitchen to get some wine. She could still taste lemon and ginger tea.

CHAPTER EIGHTEEN

Two missed calls and a voicemail from Carla waited for Sophie upon waking the next morning. Her faithful therapist checking in on her after the window banging incident the day before. That's kind of her, Sophie thought. But then she remembered: Alex's keys... Alex's keys... sounded in her head over and over, like a mantra.

Sophie didn't have to wait more than one ring when she rang her back. 'Carla, it's Sophie.'

'Oh, Sophie. Thank you for returning my call. Really, I just wanted...'

'Carla, can you tell me something? I just want to check with you because I've been going over it in my mind and if you could just tell me what I saw was real then maybe I could relax. And look, if he's your patient or anything, I understand and I know you can't really tell me...'

'Sounds like we need to make you another appointment Sophie. Would you like to come in today?'

Ignoring her question, she pressed on. 'I accidentally saw a bunch of keys in your bag and they looked a lot like my husband's and can you just tell me that he is okay?' Sophie assumed Carla's silence meant she was pondering the right thing to say.

'I have an opening in an hour. Can you make that?'

You bet Sophie could make that.

There was a line of sweat around the rim of Sophie's hair. She could smell the mustiness of her t-shirt and her unwashed body and hoped Carla wouldn't notice. Carla opened her door at 9am and stood aside with a forlorn look, an arm pointing towards the couch. 'Sophie.' She sighed and half-smiled. A thousand spiders soldiered up Sophie's throat. Whatever was coming was not going to put her at ease.

'I've got something to show you.' Carla bent over her office chair without uncrossing her ankles and snapped back up brandishing a cluster of unfamiliar keys. On it, a brand new keyring the same as Alex's weathered one. It bore a similar rose hue but had more life and polish to it. Sophie couldn't see any etchings.

'These keys are what you saw in my bag yesterday. They're mine. Do you still believe they are your husband's?'

'No, clearly not. I'm sorry... I just thought...'

'Sophie, it seems to me, in my professional opinion, which is what you are here for, right?' She didn't wait for acknowledgement. 'I think you are deteriorating. I do believe you can turn it around and get better quickly but as I see it, there have been a few more hallucinations and mental disturbances than a week ago. Would you agree?'

'No! I'm doing much better. I had the nightmare last night and I was able to go back to sleep quite quickly.' Sophie didn't know why she was lying.

'You've been having the nightmare again?'

Sophie realised her mistake.

'Sophie there's nothing frightening you have to do. I'm not suggesting you need to stay in a hospital or do anything outside of what we have been doing but I strongly advise we increase the frequency of our sessions.'

Sophie was relieved that she wasn't quite at the dreaded hospital stay stage, for that meant something more than it really was. It meant it would be harder to return to sanity whereas now she could return at any moment, living her life as she had always done before Alex left and when she had a job. It was entirely plausible, so far, in her narrative that if she could just get a decent night's sleep and wake up without the grainy burden of her mind slipping into mud, she'd be fine. Minus her husband.

'Do you think it's time I explore my options with medication? I mean, some of that Cymbalta or antipsychotics scare me a little but maybe something gentler? And some Valium?'

'No Sophie. I would encourage you to avoid all this

at all costs. I truly believe the work you and I do together will supersede your need for these types of medication and we can break through quicker without them. We're at a really crucial stage of your healing and narcotics will interfere with our progress.'

Sophie wanted to rebel and twisted her lips with her teeth, a little surprised that a health professional was advising against medication. But Carla obviously saw something that Sophie didn't so, for now, she would obey. And how could she trust her own mind as to what was right for itself when just days ago she actually thought she had the ability to fly? Sophie shuddered at the thought of flinging off the balcony onto the concrete and the people below. In the face of the alternatives, a few more sessions with Carla were not terrible. Anything to help her get back on an even keel so that when Alex eventually returned home, he would see what a capable, strong and balanced woman she was. He would be so impressed and Sophie would be so appealing, that Alex would reclaim his stake in their family and never deviate. He didn't even have to know that Sophie ever went through this unhinged phase. *And this is definitely just a phase*, she reminded herself.

Sophie left her session with Carla feeling lighter, a spring had almost found its way into her step. It was an honest mistake; two keyrings could look the same. As she came up to her car, Sophie stuck her hand in her pocket to find her keys. Her hand touched the piece of paper she found in Alex's clothes with Carla's address on it. It sat in her hand like a dead moth, reminding her of the anxiety and confusion she previously felt and she admonished herself for forgetting about it and not confronting Carla.

Looking around her, she made a split-second decision and spotting a sports clothing store, she ran into it. After a few minutes, she runs out with a new stiff cap and a heavy charcoal coloured cashmere scarf wound around her neck and hair to obscure her identity somewhat from a distance. If Alex visited Carla's office, she wanted to be able to get as close to him as possible before he recognised her. She just needed to see his face. Whatever he truly felt for her, it would be held there. If he knew that leaving was a mistake and he didn't know how to come back to her, she would see it in the droop of his eyelids, the dourness of his mouth. If he was besotted with another, his eyes could never lie. Something within her, bubbling up from the middle of her bowel wanted her to pay attention. But the more she ignored the thought, tried to reason with it, logic it away. But it was no use. The stronger she fought with it, tried to meld it into another thought, the stronger it revolted. The thought was that Alex was having an affair with Carla. He had to have been. It explained the late nights at work, the distance he put between them, the paper with her office address on it. The similarity in keyrings only compounded Sophie's belief more.

Sophie sat waiting in her parked car, near Carla's office, in amidst afternoon shoppers', in the boutique supermarket's car park. No one came or went from the office. There was certainly no sign of Alex. And Sophie's phone still remained unrung. The only movement was the increasing hurricane winding itself up inside her. The thin nights and the flaking off of her identity had left her weak; her legs and eyelids painfully heavy.

As five o'clock slipped by, Sophie had all but resigned herself to another night of mediocre wine, punishing nightmares and unanswered questions and she watched Carla, with assured hands, lock her office and slide towards her own car. The bright copper oval keyring hung from between her fingers. It was all Sophie could look at as she decided she was going to follow Carla home and confront her, and Alex, about their affair.

CHAPTER
NINETEEN

T he day was grey all around them and Sophie was desperate not to lose sight of those devil red eyes of Carla's brake lights that would lead her to wherever she was going. Home, she assumed. Sophie kept flicking her eyes back to the numbers on Carla's number plate... 'X, X, 10, 10,' she repeated over and over in case it slipped far away out of her mind. If she could just get a look at the keyring one more time, touch it, see it up close, she could be certain. If it really is new and not Alex's, I'll forget about this forever and can move on, she promised herself.

After both cars passed too many intersections and the city slipped further away, Sophie fumbled for her phone on the passenger seat, eyes still trained on Carla's car up ahead. 'Current location,' she requested from her phone, who parroted the name of the suburb that seemed only vaguely familiar. *Fuck it*, she thought. *I'm doing this*. And sat a reasonable distance from the back of Carla's car for a lot longer than seemed like a typical evening commute. When the grey cinder block buildings began to turn to dry pale yellow paddocks, Sophie was sure that Carla knew someone was following her and was just taking the piss. Making the follower drive along until they got bored or ran out of petrol.

It had been a long fruitless day for Sophie and she had convinced herself that Carla and Alex were, somehow, linked. And getting hold of that keyring would prove it, either way. The more she mentally chewed on it, the less it seemed likely that Alex was a patient. Sure, he was stressed at work the last time Sophie had seen him but nothing he couldn't manage. He certainly didn't appear to be unravelling into the state that Sophie had found herself in. The image of the two having an affair also looked starkly wrong in her mind's eye. But the relief of explanation would soothe her. Once she knew for sure. The unknown was doing nothing but fuel the hallucinations, the midnight voices and the nightly escapades that ran her dreamscape. She was drained. And any kind of answers that she could find, no matter how disturbing, would provide her with some chunk of peace that she'd been hungering for.

Ahead, Carla's red lights grew brighter as she came up to a fence on the side of the road. Sophie kept driving past her as inconspicuously as possible, her head and spine straight, like she was about to be told off in a classroom. The red eyes dimmed in her rearview mirror as they waggled their way up a hill beyond the fence.

'Current location?'

'I'm sorry,' her phone said unapologetically, 'I am having trouble with your request.'

She tried ringing Alex again for good measure but his phone repeated the same dead-end message. Sophie could not stand the thought, could not even stand being with herself, cooped up in her car without resolve. If she just went up the hill where Carla disappeared to, knocked on her door and explained herself... 'I just want to know where Alex is. Can you help me find him?' She imagined pleading. Or, if Alex answered, she would tell from his face. The answers would be etched into the lines that forked off his eyes. Plus, she'd had the total satisfaction of showing up to his little bubble and declaring that she knew exactly what he was up to. A small portion of revenge for him leaving her so abruptly.

Earlobes stinging with adrenalin, she left her car and stumbled along the fence waiting to come to an opening or a gate. She just hoped she'd see Carla's lights again when she trekked over the hill. Worn out grooves in the grass began to take the shape of a dirt road and Sophie risked her clothing and skin by pushing down the barbed wire fence and hauling a leg over at a time, careful not to release the tension of the wire up between her legs.

The triumph of saddling over the barb wire fence spurred on a little jog up an incline that she wished, although she could not actually see, would lead her to a house. Her cheeks stung and she promised herself that at the first sign of feeling too cold, she would turn back to her car, drive back through the city and all the way home to a steaming hot shower. But it was all lip service because at that moment she had started to feel really alive. Her mind broke way for a piercing, and strangely addictive, clarity. Clarity so gooey, yet sharp, that it made her shudder and nod at herself. 'Yes. Yes!' She whispered to herself. She was so glad that she'd chosen to do this.

As she stalked up the hill, her thoughts became even clearer. *I won't even really need to say anything to Alex and Carla. They will just know too! We will all just know. They will look at me and know that we're all in this together. This is just part of the process of life! Alex will come home with me, Carla will understand and relinquish him with encouragement. Alex and I will be better than ever!* Her eyesight changed from swimmy to hyper-focused like someone was adjusting a camera lens back and forth. As she discharged herself over the other side of the hill, the strange honeycomb of gentle lights of Carla's home that spread out before her were alluring.

CHAPTER TWENTY

The lights, Sophie realised as her pace slowed and she came closer, were small fires dotted in no particular pattern, flanking one large fire that had been considerately built. Logs leaning on one another, arching up towards the sky, sparks overlapping each other to get higher and higher. But the fires were not what Sophie noticed the most. Beside a large reflective shed were many white tents, surrounded by rocks and strings of flowers and herbs.

Suddenly, Sophie's thoughts lost all their clarity and began to bang into one another, like people at a busy mall. The more she tried to focus on what she was seeing below her, the more it melted into a scene that felt simultaneously recognisable and strange.

People and activity started to dance before her,

tack piano tunes hit the air and floated away before the next one rolled on coupled with the chink of mallet on steel like an echoing metronome, keeping time for all that work to a perfunctory beat. There were ropes and more ropes that all sorts of garments hung off and flapped around like seals clapping, whip cracks and hollering and the brinny of a horse collided mid-air. Despite the dark, everything seemed cased in a giant spotlight which made the fires and oil lamps and lanterns that hung from trees seem to twinkle brighter. An insect buzz of applause circled around her and her chest warmed as she felt pulled towards the pleasant chaos of the circus that spread out before her.

Hit with confusion, she touched her fingers to the dewy ground below her, trying to shake away the hallucination and root herself back into reality. And her mission to catch out Alex. But her fingers remained damp and the carnival stayed alive for a bit longer.

But then the picture fell away with the clap of someone's hands and she looked directly into the eyes of a warm faced man in his sixties. Ankles bare, his terracotta linen pants flapped on his legs as he darted towards Sophie and widening his arms in a low V shape, at hip height, leaving her questioning whether he intended to hug or hold hands or nothing at all.

'Hello there. This is a nice surprise,' the crinkle faced man said.

Sophie's eyes bounced over each grubby tent and

finally settled to the nuggety man in front of her. Standing a few metres behind him, was a smiling woman with a slight flush, a ruddy nose set against pale skin. Her smile was strongly curved but each eye looked as if pulled upwards by stage hooks.

'I'm sorry to have crashed your camp. I'm actually looking for someone's house. I must have gotten lost,' Sophie confessed.

'There are not many houses around here,' the man chuckled with his whole face. He had a rim of hair that swooped at the back of his head from ear to ear and his syrupy brown eyes didn't end. He had a fatherly energy that Sophie realised that she'd been missing her whole life.

'Oh, I...' Sophie stopped short before she revealed herself to be following someone. Stalking someone? Was that what she was doing? Did that mean, Carla was camping with these people? Was Alex here too? Impossible. He absolutely despised camping. He wouldn't even step foot in a caravan, '...because of the smell...' he claimed.

'Oh, you're so welcome here. You look cold. Come sit by the fire.' The way he spoke was tender and there was much humour in his eyes, backed up by traces of a speech impediment. He fluttered his hand enthusiastically, beckoning her to follow and perch on a well-worn stump by the fire. The silent, but sunny, woman behind him leant over her and wrapped a crocheted blanket around her shoulders. Sophie smiled in thanks and felt her toes and fingers slacken as she warmed up. The man placed his hands on her shoulders as he stood behind her. 'I'm Clive. This here is Everley. Would you like a tea or some water?'

The question was so carefully polite that Sophie felt obliged. 'Tea, please. Herbal if you have it.'

A cup of something spicy smelling swooped in front of her. Lemon and ginger. Her favourite.

'Lemon and ginger is my favourite at the moment.' Sophie glinted her eyes at Clive and then at Everley's back, who had already darted away.

'We know.' She thought Clive said as she fell into a crevice of headachey darkness.

CHAPTER
TWENTY ONE

'Morningstar time! Morningstar time!'
Sophie awoke to the chirrup around
her but felt weighed down by stones
and as if her entire skeleton had been replaced
with iron overnight. A smile appeared near her
half-open eyes. 'Morningstar is here. No need to
move. Everything is okay. You might have a little
headache. I have something for that, I'll give you
in a bit.' Everley, with her cold-blushed flesh, was
kneeling beside her in the faint daylight. Sophie's
neck stung as she twisted it slowly and tried to lift
her heavy torso from the burlap sack she lay upon.
Pressing her shoulders back down, Everley said,
'no need to get up yet, just lay a bit longer.'
Sophie's hands scrambled around her body, touching the crocheted rugs that housed her, feeling her
legs to notice she still had all her clothes from last

night.

'Oh sweetheart, no need to panic. You're safe. You must have passed out. Exhaustion, I'd say. My sister once had exhaustion so bad that she started to wet herself all the time and then when she went to lay down once, she couldn't get out of bed for six days! I had to bring her cereal all through the day and shove the spoon in, so she'd eat. She wasn't talking much. She was fine after all, though. Truly, she just needed a good long rest. Anyway, just rest. We'll look after you.' More smiles.

'I should go home really. My car... I should see a doctor.' *Or at least be home in my own bed if I'm suffering from some sort of exhaustion incident,* Sophie thought. A fatigue collapse was not entirely unfeasible since she had scarcely slept in countless days. Sophie remembered then that yesterday (was it actually only yesterday?) she forgot to eat as she shivered outside Carla's office for the day. Annoyance rose up.

'That's okay, we have a nurse onsite. She'll look after you until you feel well enough to get back to your car. Or we can drive you home. Have some water.'

The water was a metallic slap on her tongue and she could finally open her eyes wide enough to look at the cherubic features before her. Never had there been a more comforting face and she passed back the anodised cup with gratitude, letting her hand linger a little on the warmth of her hand.

'Good girl.' She tapped Sophie's knee, beamed

stronger and turned away, pushing open two sheets of canvas which revealed a dim light of morning outside. Sophie looked around the compact tent she had found herself in. There was barely room for the two women but Sophie lay on a makeshift bed which was too narrow to roll over in and was capped with a significant pile of crocheted rugs. If she stretched her feet out, she would knock them over. The floor was concealed under a faded Persian rug that Sophie assumed lay flush against the dirt; the smell of fresh earth came at her. It was unusually cosy, the mass of the blankets and warmth had really settled in her bones and she realised that she was, in fact, utterly exhausted. It was taking effort to stay awake. If she was forced to run right at that second, she doubted her legs would even work.

Despite being groggy, she is aware she must get up and try to find Alex. Sensing hushed but present activity outside the tent, Sophie conjured her unwilling legs over the side of the bed, noticing the hardness as she pushed her palm into its side to help her movement. She patted down the side of her half numb thighs to find her phone but came up empty. Her hand swished beneath the blankets but still didn't find her phone. *Shit, I must have left it in the car,* she panicked.

By the time she woozily forced herself outside the tent flaps, unsteady and precariously slow on her frozen legs, morning had definitely begun according to the clamour of birds that were celebrating in surround sound. Although she had detected some commotion in the camp, she had not prepared for what she saw.

About a dozen women turned to her with wide smiles, each mid-task, with something in their hands. One was hanging out pieces of pallid fabric. One had an armful of firewood and another a small blackened copper saucepan which steam escaped from. And one petite woman was perched on a fire stump and was crocheting fast and hard, her eyes locked on Sophie. Each wore an off-white windcheater. Some paired it with matching tracksuit pants, some with claret coloured fishing pants or stretched out leggings. There were one or two jumpers that were obviously newer and some were stretched at the bottom or pushed up past their elbows so the material billowed out like gigot sleeves.

Sophie trod carefully—as much as her heavy legs seemed to allow— and made an awkward 'ha' sound towards the closest woman. 'Did I crash a reunion or something?'

Most of the women tittered around her in a circular echo. Like the birds, Sophie thought. 'Quite like that, yes. We are a "re"-union of sorts.'

'I didn't mean to intrude! Thanks so much for looking after me last night. It's appreciated. I'll probably head to my car now and go straight to a hospital. Yes, I think that's best,' Sophie croaked without enthusiasm.

'At least stay for breakfast? Jenny does a really

good damper that you'll love! Assuming you're not vegan or anything?'

Sophie tried to giggle but found that she couldn't. 'Not vegan.'

'Well then! We'd love you to join us. It would also make us feel better knowing you are well enough to see yourself home.'

Sophie sat down and smacked at her thighs trying to get some feeling back, whilst two of the women smile creepily at her. Even in the gentle sun, she couldn't get any proper feeling back in her legs.

The sharp laugh of Clive from somewhere in the heart of the largest tent intruded and Sophie was reminded of Alex. Some breakfast would give her the strength to walk a little further— she must have been only off by a few hundred metres—and surprise Carla. And maybe Alex. She pictured Carla opening the door, her curly hair wound tighter around her face, a pair of flannelette pyjamas with some kitschy clouds or sheep on them, each button fastened. Complemented by fluffy slippers. Or was she the type to get up extra early and Sophie would greet her on the front stoop, stretching her hamstrings after her daily jog? Alex would be in the kitchen, dutifully making her coffee and absently looking out the window, wondering if he could surprise Carla with some morning sex. Sophie merely a memory that was leaving him more and more each day. The imagined scenes made Sophie's stomach feel like the smouldering coal that lay near her feet. So, she looked across to the woman who offered her a small bowl of food and nodded simply, as Everley came up and wrapped a blanket around her like a cape.

The women were birds, swooping with their crocheted wings to sweep Sophie around, wherever they thought she should be. It had been a long time since anyone had taken Sophie under their wing and it was too enticing not to enjoy, if only for the morning. As she pulled the ends of the blanket towards each other to cover her chest, she noticed the jumpers of the women all had a black "X" printed on the front.

Sophie listened to a single magpie warbling close by. The rolling gargle made her feel unhurried and despite herself, she dozed again as the women silently and diligently worked around her.

Sophie came to, hearing the women of the camp stirring with pots clanging, laughter and benign chatter that all had its own saccharine cadence. A softness to the edge of their words that felt surreal. Like a meditation recording was playing on repeat. It felt like a tonic, compared to the harried noise of her mind recently.

'Oh, you poor, poor thing,' concern washed Clive's face out and he lightly held Sophie's hand as he suddenly appeared in front of her again. His metallic breath swished around her.

'You're okay, my dear. You've just had a bit of a spill. We're taking good care of you. You're going to be okay.' He sat down beside her and sipped his tea out of a vintage floral teacup, which looked oddly out of place there in the middle of the woods.

The campsite in the clearing looked different during the afternoon, once the bleariness of the morning had worn off. It looked like a completely new world in the daylight. Stationed behind the ring of tents and pushed back all the way until it looked like it was part of the woods, was an enormous enclosed hay shed. It was wide enough to house two tractors, side by side and Sophie couldn't gauge how long it was from where she was sitting. There were no windows, no holes and no visible openings. The shed looked reasonably new and the shiny aluminium clashed against the weathered tents. It was hard not to look at and pulled focus away from other more intriguing sights, such as the raging bonfire and the collection of disjointed people that were dotted around the encampment.

Clive emanated warmth, not just a temperature, but a kind of aura that felt like golden syrup. Despite herself, Sophie felt it permeate her every cell and her body begged her to surrender to a deep relaxation, like lying in the bursting sun on a cool day. If she was honest with herself, she'd say that it was the first time that she had ever felt taken care of and relaxed and there was something ever so appealing about the experience. However, there was another, more rigid, part of her mind that reminded her that these people were strangers and she was quite possibly very ill. Physically and mentally.

'Do you have any idea when you can help me get

back to my car?' Sophie asked flatly.

'We thought it best that our nurse check you out first and then we'll walk you back to your car, if that's okay? Just to be safe. She's just returning from the city and should be back any minute.'

It made sense to Sophie. So she relaxed a little and took in her surroundings properly. 'What's beyond here?' She pointed in the direction of where she believed Carla's house— and possible where Alex— was.

'Well, not much really. More woods.'

'Oh,' she said disappointed.

Although there was a denser ring of trees around the clearing, near the fire were intermittent clusters of trees, with collections of limestone piled at the base of the trunk. Fallen branches lay below them like soldiers. There was junk piled up at nearly every tree: heavy chains rusted so much they were almost black, hanging from trees all lined up so they formed a blanket. Half-formed animal skulls— perhaps for decoration or intimidation, or both. Sophie scanned her eyes across the other collected debris: a cast iron pot swinging in the mild wind like a pendulum and circles of iron, like hoops or bangles positioned on the arm of a tree stump. One tree proudly displayed a rusted wagon wheel— the epitome of a world gone to the past.

Swallows dived like hang gliders, a movementless glide, dipping diagonally where the sharp ledge of the front of their wings sliced through air supported by invisible forces. Flashes of red and green captured her eyesight as they tilted their small bodies back and forth, in what would otherwise be an ordinary afternoon.

Taking it all in, she observed those around her. None of the women spoke to her or even acknowledged her. She felt like she didn't exist again. A resurgence of Ghost Girl. Like she was an elderly woman at a country football match, freezing away the afternoon. Occasionally, she would catch people looking at her from a distance but they would divert their eyes so quickly, without pausing their duties, that she wasn't sure if they were really looking at all. No one was close enough that Sophie could tell what their eyes were doing without distortion.

As if reading her mind, Clive smiled at her and said 'I see you, you know.' He continued to smile and sipped on tea in a metal cup beside her. Sophie wasn't quite sure what he meant but didn't want to break the spell. 'You're not invisible to us. Your greatness, your potentiality, it's all very obvious. Perhaps cos we are strangers to you, perhaps because we aren't burdened by the distraction of the world and we spend our time refining what we see so that we can easily spot perfection when it is thrust upon us.'

Sophie delicately scoffed, 'I'm far from perfect. In fact, I'm completely the opposite. I'm a dysfunctional mess who her husband can't stand to be around.' The effort of complete sentences heightened her weariness.

'Yes, that is what your mind is telling you, my dear. But it might not be the truth. Consider that, although unknown to you, this group of people could very well know exactly what they see when they see it. I'm sixty years old, do you think I have no wisdom?'

'I don't mean to imply that. I know myself quite well and... I just want to get back to being normal. Like I was before.'

'Before what exactly?' He whispered his question and the sound of his mouth moving tinkled.

'Before I turned thirty and started getting a bit wobbly in the head. And then definitely before Alex, my husband, left. Things were fine then. If only...' She trailed off, unsure why she was revealing herself to a stranger. Was it the exhaustion?

'Sophie, often the Universe is giving us a great gift by pushing us one way or the other, even if it pushes us into great discomfort. Consider that it has all happened for a reason. And if you truly look at it, get wildly honest with yourself, were things truly fine? Or is it a case of peering back over our past with rose coloured glasses?'

An intense hatred rose in Sophie. How dare this man who knew nothing about her cast such pedestrian assertions. 'Actually, I'm quite aware that things were fine, thank you. Not everything is a moment to be analysed.'

'If you say so. I believe you.' He leant closer to her and blinked slowly and her annoyance slipped away quietly, replaced by the familiar lethargy.

Like a tag team, Everley came back and Clive slid away.

'Sophie, I'm so sorry to tell you this. I know you're keen to get home but our nurse is running a little late. She shouldn't be too far off,' Everley claimed, embarrassment creeping up her face.

Promising an early dinner as compensation for the delay in the nurse returning from the city, Everley helped Sophie to her feet, one of which was encased in pins and needles, like she had stepped on an echidna's back. With her arm slung around Everley's sharp shoulders, Sophie was shuffled carefully towards the big shed. She could not deny that she was ravenous. The thought of food lured her more than her desire to find Alex in that moment.

As she was unhurriedly moved to the shed, Sophie had time to take in her surroundings even more. To the side of the shed, a little obscured from the rest of the camp, was an enormous herb garden. Sophie looked across it in awe, with its glistening array of greys, lavender and olive coloured plants. Rows and rows of sage, wormwood, wild fennel, mint, lemon balm, borage and clumps of aloe vera in each corner. Everywhere, mandrake plants held the family of herbs together. There were small pink salvia flowers that smelt like passionfruit and cinnamon made the air rich with its potency. Lavender bushes stood to attention, like grey soldiers, begging to be knocked down. Furry leaves of sage brushed at Sophie's calves in her imagination begging to be crushed between her fingers. The garden was divided into smaller rectangles to allow for walking paths in between the rows of perfectly lined up plants, all sectioned with hedges of rosemary. In the centre of the herb garden sat a wide copper birdbath, green with age. The birdbath was the size of a wagon wheel and nearly as tall as Sophie. She could hear it hum against the motion of the breeze and she yearned to climb up into it and wash herself clean. Birds darted back and forth, to seek their rewards as the herbs stood guard for the birdbath. There were tiny little wooden signs that ended each row. Mint: make something brand new again. Basil: potent for money, Rosemary: protection and cleansing. There was even an adorable little sign under the huge pregnant orange tree that read: Orange blossom: propel wishes. The garden was heady with scent which transported her far away, out of her body and into a place where she was safe and not riddled with the emotional torment of being abandoned by her one true love. The smell was a comfort and a frustration; for the barely-there scent of the plants wafted over the breeze like a ghost catching flight and it reminded Sophie of something that she could not grasp. Somewhere she had been before. But her mind circled around and around and could not land on the place where she had been. It was like having a déjà vu but not being able to remember what the déjà vu was about. Sophie slowed her shuffling down, enough that she could feel Everley tugging at her with impatience. Her head swam and she wanted to lay down in between the shrubs and watch the honeyeaters and the robins dance across her eyesight, minding their business. As she gave in to Everley's gentle tugs and hastened her pace towards the shed, she realised two things. The shed and herb garden gave something away: that these people lived here. It wasn't just a campground for the weekend, it was their home. And secondly, she realised the smell of the herbs that had entranced her, it did so for a reason. It made her feel like she was home too.

CHAPTER
TWENTY TWO

'Before the sermon, we simply must feast!' One of the men, Jesse, pulled back the sliding shed door like a magician pulling back a curtain to reveal a trick as Everley and Sophie approached. The shed seemed to go back like a tunnel and Sophie was in awe at the paraphernalia that lined the walls. In the middle of the shed, sat a long wooden table which was cluttered with a variety of overflowing bowls of a mish-mash of salads, dotted with condiments, plates heavy with thick meats in shades of grey, white and pink. Weaving around the plates were swarms of roots, parted by thin white candles.

The group rushed in behind her as one, clapping their hands with joy, arms entwined, a vibrancy in the air that was almost infectious enough for Sophie to catch. If she'd let herself. She didn't realise how hungry she was until she saw the luscious green leaves of lettuces laid around a bowl, shiny with oil and holding sliced boiled eggs that were covered in a greying dressing.

'Come on in!' Clive's baron-like voice boomed through the shed, drawing the group in and echoing around them until everyone found a place. Oversized mugs of steaming tea were passed around as Everley was stationed at a large porcelain urn, administering the tea to all who asked.

'Right, everyone in?' Clive checked. When there were no protests, he stood up pushing his chair back with the sinewy hard bit of the back of his thighs. Holding a candle, he jigged his way up to a large wreath that hung from the back wall of the shed. With a flourish, he lit the wreath which went up in fierce flames, in a matter of two seconds. Everyone cheered at the fiery display and began ravenously stabbing their plates with forks. Sophie watched as the wreath dripped burnt bits to the floor, nothing remaining except a bare blackened bit of wire. She wanted to get lost in the fantastical celebration of it all but the twist in her gut, that she had inherited since Alex left, would not unravel.

'Sshh. He's about to start.' One of the pointy men aggressively stated to two women who were whispering, hunched over the remains of their salad. The spicy scent of the herb garden breezed in around them.

Clive bounced up to a gap at the top of the table.

Sophie had watched people earlier in the day move in a makeshift stage, which was nothing more than rudimentary steps and a small platform that jutted out, a metre off the ground. Made from plywood, it looked as unsteady as it did ridiculous against the backdrop of the cluttered shed.

Clive jogged up the steps, clapped his hands together and looked to the ceiling, keeping his hands at his chest. It was the first time that Sophie had seen anyone in the camp not don one of the hideous outdated jumpers. He wore black cargo pants and a white cheesecloth shirt, despite the chill, and looked like he could be taking a European vacation, not living out in the middle of a paddock. 'Ahhhhh.' Clive looked around at the faces that beamed up at him, while a few people shuffled around, getting comfortable, swaying their spines from side to side, wrapping excess shawls around then, reaching for one anothers' hands. They were preparing themselves to listen, Sophie noticed. They wanted to hear whatever was about to happen.

'What a glorious time is thrust upon us!' He began. A chorus of 'Venus is...' echoed throughout the watchers. Sophie felt uneasy. Who was Venus?

'Some people, those that live in the city or other parts of the world, might believe that what we do here, what we believe, what we know to be true, is a little... kooky.' The watchers laughed.

'And that is okay. I honour all those that question their truths. But we're living together because we are preparing together. We all share a unique vision that we have been blessed with that not many of this world have been privy to. And for that, we must be grateful. Do you agree?' Clive smiled at a few people looking up at him, avoiding Sophie at all costs.

Something dropped with a clunk in her stomach. Nausea curled up like steam from the pit of her stomach as she watched everyone in the shed eat up Clive's words. They all looked hungry and weak, for something that wasn't food.

'And we must forgive these people that think ill of us. For they haven't been blessed with the visions of The New Way. The very same people that will one day come to rely on us or perish. And we will welcome them and forgive them with the heart of elephants. Will we not? For who here has received welcoming and forgiveness at a time when they needed it the most?' The circle erupted into applause and cheers.

'Let's hear your story one more time Jesse? Tell us of your salvation and forgiveness to remind us that everything can change for us quickly, if we allow it.'

Jesse skipped up to the steps. 'Most of you know my story. Have heard it many times. But there's never a dip in joy when I tell it again. Some of you have said that you get a lot out of hearing it again. So here goes.' Jesse awkwardly pulled the sleeves over his hands and blew into his cupped hands, whilst dancing from barefoot to barefoot.

'A few years ago... I think two now?' Jesse looked to Clive for confirmation, which he nodded back. 'I was plagued by these horrendous nightmares. No matter what I would do— smoke weed, drink, stay awake, meditation, exercise like a fiend—they would roll through me every night. I couldn't shake them. They seemed to have come out of nowhere and when they took hold they just wouldn't let me go. I think I even tried drinking nothing by apple juice for five days straight cos I read somewhere... you get the idea.' He rolled his eyes at himself. 'These horrid nightmares always featured my skin peeling off. It would just kinda fall off. Not in chunks but pretty much in one or two big sheets, starting at the face. I would see these sheets of skin lying in front of me, the colour of bloody puss. I never knew what to do about the sheets of skin or how to be without skin. I couldn't bear to look at myself in case I was just blood and muscles.' He shuddered. 'Ohhh. I still feel sick thinking about them. I know that reoccurring nightmares are pretty common, right?' He looked around at the faces before him and nodded back at a few sharp 'yeps' from his audience. Sophie may not have been entirely comfortable at this unusual dinner party but at least she could relate to the agony of unrelenting nightmares.

'So anyway. One day I got talking to our man Clive here in the bookstore, of all places. It wasn't so much what Clive said to me but the way he said it and, mainly, the way I felt when I looked at him.

I saw something that the nightmares had been clouding. I saw hope and faith. I lost hope and I had lost faith and without those two ingredients, I was eating a shit pie... if you like.' He sniggered at his own joke. Sophie was surprised that others found it funny.

A sweet young woman, who Sophie heard Everley call Abigail earlier, perched up higher than the others on a chair a little outside the circle. Her back was straight and she had a cream bonnet tied underneath her chin, that looked positively antique. If it wasn't for the signature jumper she wore, Sophie would swear she had escaped from the past or from an Amish settlement. Abigail paid attention to every word spoken, listening intently, but did not engage. She did not laugh when others did nor nod in agreement. Sophie found consolation in her insubordinate stillness.

Jesse continued. 'Although a bit shy at first— understandably of course since I was just a stranger who worked in a bookstore and didn't know what he was doing with his life— Clive eventually was gracious enough to let me know about The New Way. And I was never more ready than I was when I came here and met you all. You welcomed me like I had never been welcomed in my life. I finally felt at home and like I had something that was guiding me. And everything that had happened in my life, everything that I had done or not done, had finally made sense. Like there was a reason for all of it. And I felt like I finally had a purpose and that I was not a rudderless boat on a fast stream anymore. I had arrived. And of course, the very first night I came here, my nightmares ceased and I haven't had one since.' Jesse paused, triumphantly, and beamed at everyone, including Sophie. Most people, except Sophie, burst into applause. Even Abigail tapped one pale hand on her thigh insipidly as a token gesture.

'Thank you,' Jesse held a hand to his heart and used the other hand to tuck his shoulder-length tatty hair behind his ears. He looked like a smug rat in the light of the fire, his beady eyes pleased at the attention and his nose pointy enough to be used as an exclamation point on his speech.

Clive retook his position on the stage and embraced Jesse in a long hug. From the way their fingers pressed into each others' backs, Sophie could tell the men were gripping each other hard. To Sophie, it looked uncomfortably hard.

'Isn't that just one of our favourite stories?'

'Yeah!' Again, Abigail barely move her lips.

'Now, it's that time! The time we have all been waiting for. Let's get to it, shall we?'

Everley, who sat the closest to the stage clapped her hands with childlike glee.

'You all know the rules, try not to ask the same question over and over again, wait your turn, your question will be answered whether you ask it or not. And so on. And goodnight...!' Clive stood completely still, his feet wide apart and his hands clasped in front of him. He shut his eyes and began rocking slightly from side to side. Abigail was the only one that shut her eyes with him. After what felt like half an hour to Sophie, Clive popped his eyes open and declared it was time to begin. Sophie could taste what was coming and it tasted like off milk.

'Let us commune with the spirit of us and the energy of Planet Venus and its occupants, those that can speak and those that cannot. For we are all learners and on a path to being at one with you. We are ready.' He nodded to himself. 'Before I open to any questions, there are some things I must share with you.

It is crucial that you realise that these are not my words, not the words of a Senior who is starting to shrivel as an old man,' he giggled. 'But words that come from a realm that you are yet to experience but you are on your way to. These words are translated from us through the being that is Clive and it is their meaning that is important.'

Clive dropped his chin and closed his eyes but Sophie could read the smugness like he was the daily newspaper. An uneasiness started to surge inside of her. Did Clive really believe he was an alien from Venus? Or channelling them? That kind of delusion was all too familiar in Sophie's world and it repulsed her for it was the very thing she had been trying to skirt away from for months. Insanity and delusion, two best friends, who had been begging her to come out and play that she was finding harder to ignore. And here they were, presenting themselves onstage to her. Seemingly revered, nonetheless.

As if reading her thoughts, Clive looked up and pointed to Sophie. 'You have recently experienced your soul crack, yes?'

Sophie turned her head away from Clive's pointed stare and rolled her eyes at no one.

'Indeed. It seems so.' He confirmed.

Sophie mumbled under her breath which did not deter Clive in the slightest, for he was on a roll. He bounced slightly on the balls of his feet but the top half of him remained steady and focussed. 'As people, you are so fragile. It's wonderful that you are. Truly. You were made that way. The fragility causes the soul crack that you have all experienced at some point or are susceptible to one. We're sorry you had to go through that. It is ugly. Have it be known that your fragility is your superpower. It's what makes you. It's what creates you. It's what you created out of. This fragility— and I really want you to ponder and meditate on it— this fragility is a special kind of magic. Float away with it. People will love you for it. Some bastards— as you humans would say— will take advantage of it because that is the only way they know how to interact with it. They are not skilled or advanced enough to handle or live with another's fragility unless they are soaking it up and destroying it. Like a flower, they have an impulse to smash it up and pull the petals off. Rather than lovingly admire it, take care of it, be fuelled by its beauty.

Again, be assured that on Venus, fragility is celebrated, worshipped and encouraged. Please cultivate your fragility now so as to not harm other lifeforms when our planets join in harmony.' Clive dumped his hands to his side, which signalled he was done with his discourse. 'And now... questions?'

Eager hands shot upward, even before he finished the word. Clive spread his arms wide and his head bobbed. As quickly as the hands were raised, his struck out, like a cobra and pointed to a man sitting next to Everley who had just sat down after handing out more cups of tea. She was flushed with delight from her duty.

'Please, will you speak of Venus?' The man queried and shuffled excitedly.

'It would be an honour. The planet Venus welcomes you as one of our own. The conditions are different than what you are used to there on Earth, with all its density and physicality and, most of the time, its depravity. Just like leaving your home when you go on vacation, you must leave earthly ways behind when you embark Venus. Although the planets will be joined, there will only be one way and that is The New Way of Planet Venus. For it is stronger, more powerful and it holds a magnetic field that is at a higher frequency than that of Planet Earth's. The density will fall away and the lightness of Venus will burn, like a bushfire, that of Earth's. We do not wish to destroy your glorious abode but the damage has already been done. Those that have been seeking to enhance their vibration and have prepared so, will be willing and fitting for the frequency that our dear planet possesses. There are things that weigh you down. Your attachment to things, to places you call home, to people you think you belong to —' Sophie could feel Clive's eyes bore into her— '... and ways of being. It is all futile in The New Way and the sooner you can discard those peacefully, without yanking it from your existence like pulling clumps of hair from your head, the better and easier you will transition.'

Another questioner was called upon rapidly. 'My question is... ohh... I'm strangely nervous. Is it going to hurt when Venus comes for us?' A mousy woman twittered.

'Firstly, I can say it will be a more natural feeling and experience and more long-lasting and thus much more satisfying and safe than your current experience. But you need to prevent yourself from seeking the fireworks and the sleepless nights of tingles that could come from melding with The New Way. Those "Hollywood" feelings. I can see you expect great, monumental things. A candy land where you are in constant orgasm. You must circumnavigate these preconceptions at once. For everything about The New Way will feel nothing short of natural. With the correct preparation, of course. Preparation, as led by those you see around you now, is the key to mitigating culture shock and will ensure you step fully into your fullness of bliss, without any raw adjustment. Venus is.'

Again, hands shot up before he finished. Another hand was picked from the sticks. 'Please, can you tell us about prophecy?'

Clive hesitated and Sophie watched with spite at the thought that something had choked him and his charade would have to stop. A little fire of rage and objection burnt inside her. This man knew nothing of personal situations and his advice seemed a little more than harmful. But she'd gorged herself on the slow-roasted pork and potatoes and had become weary again, her limbs heavy. Things were getting a little peculiar so she promised herself tomorrow, she would arrange a lift back to the city. Even if she had to beg every person in the camp. Besides, she had another appointment with Carla scheduled. Sophie wondered if she would confess to watching and following her.

As Clive's words danced on, Sophie watched as everyone seemed to warm right up. Even the thin girl, Abigail, was smiling with her lips pressed into her knuckles.

'Please. More questions?'

Sophie scoffed and heads snapped around to her. 'Where's my husband then?' Out of the corner of her eye, she could see Jesse shake his head at her.

'Great question my dear. Although we often don't use The Talk for such nugatory matters, I can tell this is causing you great anguish. And we're not friends with anguish. So, first, let me ask you a question. When was the last time you saw your husband?'

Sophie really had to think. 'Err... six weeks ago.' Sophie hoped she was right. The exhaustion and befuddlement of the ordeal had left her for wanting to keep track of days and such mundanity like using a calendar.

'I see. And we hate to be cryptic here but we want to say to you that sometimes things that do not want to be found will remain lost. Until they are ready to be found again.' Clive raised an eyebrow at her.

Sophie swore he was trying to make a point. 'So, you don't know?'

Clive's face set hard and went to launch into an attack when he turned a corner with his performance. 'Wait, wait... stop now. Something's happening,' Clive extended a palm and shook it out in front of him. Looking at the ground, he paused for an uncomfortably long time. Long enough for people to grab one another's shoulders in anticipation. Sophie noticed that Everley even had time to lay a few cylinders of wood on the big fire outside the shed. As she did the fire popped so loudly that it made everyone, especially Sophie, jump. With the fright, a few people shouted in glee. Taking advantage of the timing, Clive let it rip. 'Yehhawww!' Clive sounded like a deranged cowboy. 'Here it is. It's coming. Venus wants us to get a taste.'

Things were building and getting feverish. People were no longer happy to stay seated, some pouncing on their haunches, bouncing their backside up and down with excitement. Jesse tipped a cup of water over his face and shook it off. One woman had her eyes closed and was dancing to an imaginary beat. Sophie watched the warm light across one side of Abigail's face and even she was glistening with excitement, her eyes thick with water about to spill over her eyelashes.

'Feel it! All y'all feel it!' Clive repeatedly scooped his hands up towards the sky, like he was throwing marbles. 'I urge thee to feel it and rejoice in the bliss that is our destiny. Can you feel it?' The circle before him whooped in response and Sophie had no doubt that their feelings of elation were genuine, just manufactured rather than some divine ecstasy. Clive admired his handiwork of the frenzy before him and it was then that Sophie realised it was all fake, just as she suspected. She saw it in his face, he was so thrilled with himself that it made her nauseous. He caught her watching him and even the thrill of the party, which danced like fairies about him, couldn't stop the crushing disappointment of being caught. He flicked his eyes away from Sophie, pretending that he hadn't seen her and threw himself into a forced grin, grabbing Jesse and twirling him around in a waltz. Sophie waited for him to shut the evening down. But the end of his tirade did not seem close. Perhaps he was putting on an extra show for Sophie but he jumped off the front of the stage and landed on bent knees like a cat. Grabbing the front collar of his shirt with both hands, he yanked down hard and his shirt stretched open, revealing his surprisingly smooth chest.

'Hear the rumble of the Venus alchemy forming, like a cloud rolling together in time to spit thunder,' Clive shouted at them. 'Listen to the Seniors who prove themselves for you time and time again, the means to The New Way through the cultivation of alchemy. They do not guide you wrong. Have they yet? No, you will see that they have not. There is no room for questioning their leadership or their expectations, when they know the way.'

Sophie wondered if the routine was as transparent to others as it was to her. Cricking her neck, she looked around to the entrance, which was now gone. The shed door had been shut tight against the night. All of a sudden, Sophie felt claustrophobic and the campers' antics were no longer just amusing.

'He's a shaman you know. A powerful one at that.' A wispy woman leant over and mumbled at Sophie conspiratorially. 'I don't like to say the word "cure" but I'm sure he had something to do with my health improving.' She sucked at her lips, Sophie was too stuck in the middle of politeness and panic to shift away so she sat silently, tensing up and willing the woman with her crunchy hair and embroidered on butterflies to find another distraction. 'I had cancer you see. I can tell you this, I don't mind. Yeah, breast cancer. Last check-up, told me it was gone! Can you believe that? I'm certain that he had something to do with it.' She stabbed a fist in his direction. Sophie was put off by the woman and willed the evening to end so she could collapse in her small bed and it would be closer to a time when she could get back home. Just a little sleep and then she would walk on her own back towards her car at the first light.

But the woman persisted. 'Yeah, he does 'mazing things, let me tell you. Helped some kid walk again, apparently. I've never seen the kid but that's what a lot of these people here have told me. There must be summin in it, ya know?'

Clive had quietened down and sat at the edge of the stage with his legs swinging. One by one, the campers sat down, flushed and sweaty but silent. Some lay with a thud to the ground, as if it were a yoga class. Two women lay in another woman's lap, each taking a thigh for a pillow.

In a melodic voice, Clive said 'notice how tired you are right now. It's because you are relaxed. Your soul is releasing tension and there's an unwinding. You no longer need to be on high alert because you're uncovering the truth. Of where your true home is. And what you must do to prepare. Sink into it. 'Relax...' he swept his hand around the room. 'Relax...' his voice fell to a murmur. 'Relax.'

Sophie resisted his words and the absurdity of this man and his pathetic brainwashed followers. But she could not deny that some part of her was still listening to Clive. She had been pining to truly relax ever since she turned thirty.

She finally yanked her arm free from the woman next to her and stood up to leave. As she stood, she fainted.

CHAPTER TWENTY THREE

The banging shot through Sophie's sleep. Moving from the shed to her bed was a muffled memory. Had she been asleep hours or minutes? Abigail, her face rimmed with her bonnet, was peering down on her. 'Come on, he has summoned us again.' She put out a hand, which Sophie reluctantly took and instantly tumbled onto the floor, almost dragging Abigail with her. 'I'm sorry, I mustn't be awake properly.'

'Never mind. Everley and I shall lift you.' The two appeared at her side like doves.

'Can I perhaps just stay in bed and sleep? I'm awfully tired.' Her own words sounded underwater.

'You can but what if he has information about your husband?'

Sophie allowed the two to scoop their arms under her thighs and carry her out towards the fire. The fire was low, just a tidy pile of red coals. Around it were tall torches poking out of the ground, small flames wavering whilst they waited. The atmosphere was jubilant, confirmed by the hand drumming and eruptive laughter that filled the place with noise. Despite her aching tiredness, there was a magnetic quality to the campers' reactions. Had they been up since the dinner? It reminded Sophie of childcare, where kids were busy like ants, indulging in their choice of play. Swirling paints with their fingers just for the heck of it and declaring that it is a rainbow over and over again. Or building towers with blocks for the sheer delight of smashing them down. Repeating animal noises just to hear how they sound coming from their damp mouths.

'Is he gunna have another go at one of his so-called sermons?' Sophie boldly asked Abigail.

Taken aback she replied, 'oh no, this is the Wild Woman Ceremony. You're going to love it!'

'Oh Christ, this sounds positively gag-worthy.' And she sighed a long heavy sigh, letting her arms flop to the sides of her body.

Abigail shot her a look of confusion and then moved away to gather an armful of sticks. Sophie surprised herself when she felt a bit of relief when Abigail silently returned to her spot next to her.

Clive declared the Wild Woman Ceremony to begin and the campers gleefully and dutifully wove their sticks— mandrake and oat tree roots— around each other. No one bothered to offer Sophie some, which she was secretly pleased about but she was bored so she watched Abigail, who was weaving her roots carefully, with an intensity of a student sitting exams. When she'd finished, she held up a small, complicated wreath to show Sophie. 'See?' She said with pride.

'Oh. What is it?'

'A Mandrake root wreath. We make them in offering to the Wild Woman so she doesn't lead us to hell.'

'Symbolically, yeah?'

'Whatever do you mean? The Wild Woman lives in the woods. She's real. I've seen her.'

'Oh, come off it.'

'It's true! Do you say that I lie?'

'I say that it could have been anything at all and the imagination loves to turn it into a scary thing. That is something I know to be true.'

'Well, I saw her and her lights. Over that way,' she pointed beyond the big shed.

'Is she like a real person? A neighbour or...'

Abigail clutched her arm. 'No! You absolutely must be afraid of her! She is the woman that lives in the woods and is the guardian of the sky, the ground and the sea and the one you shall find at crossroads. A true night wanderer, she will lead you astray or take you directly to riches at her will. As mortals, it is hard to say how to best please her or disappoint her but we try.' Everley nodded along beside Abigail.

Clive overhead and sidled up next to the women

and continued Abigail's warning. 'We must never say her name for that will summon her but we must respect and fear her as much as we need to, for she is the keeper of the dark in the woods and has the power to break us or illuminate us, at her desire. If we do not please her in a way of her choosing, she will keenly and unremorsefully lead us into the underworld where she will leave us to die a thousand times and live a thousand times more in a hell that is worse than that of our own creation. If we somehow please her, she will help us transition well to The New Way when Venus connects us. You must never, NEVER, go into the woods alone at daybreak or dusk for that is when she roams and will reflect her enticing light back at you. Without preparation and appeasing, which you clearly have not get done, she will most certainly drop you down to the underworld. And I just don't like your chances, no matter how special you are. Although, truth be told, the Wild Woman is in all of us. Existing in the dark, blackest parts of our mind, waiting to guide us gently back into the day when we have lost our way through the woods of our thoughts. I will tell you though, she is to be feared. Because without warning, she will drag you down by the skin into the layers of hell. Without mercy too, for she doesn't get attached to your emotions or hear your pleas for help. Her call of judgement is one that is perfunctory and seemingly callous but who are we to judge what she judges? We cannot be both the judged and the judge. We, in our infancy and nobility of mind, in our denseness of energy, of our limited foresight, even those with the gift of prophecy, do not know enough to know the difference between what is right and what is wrong when it comes to deciding the pathway at the crossroads. So...' he continued passionately, as a few others had tuned in, '...if you cross her at the wrong time, when we have not offered enough, she will slice your throat with her thumbnail and you will bleed your unholy and un-prepared blood into the soil below you and will be eaten by the wood mice until you are nothing but empty, bleached bones.' Clive was spitting and his veins stood up in his hands, which were shaped like claws as he warned against the supposed Wild Woman.

Sophie laughed at the delusional fairy tale he was telling. She wondered how much more of this non-sense Clive had stored up inside him.

'Silence!' Clive clapped his hands for attention which brought everyone to an abrupt halt. They all rose and stood in a misshapen circle at the edge of the clearing, all facing outwards into the surrounding woods. And like confetti falling, one by one the circle members started repeating the words 'for you, for you' in a melodic and eerie chant. Some held out their wreaths in front of them and some wore wigs fashioned from tree roots, leaves and twigs. Sophie turned to quiz Abigail, but she too had absconded to be part of the circle.

Sophie looked down at her wearied body and pitied herself, her heart and face sinking. Here she was, away from home and alone, in a circle of utter weirdos who were shouting at trees. But her despair wouldn't last for long because the weird legend about the imaginary woman in the woods was the least she had to worry about.

CHAPTER
TWENTY FOUR

S ophie woke up the next morning but was too exhausted and weak to move, her eyelids too thick to open fully. Weary distress kept threatening to drag her under as she tried to shout for help which came out no louder than a cat's meow.

Through her half-open lids, she spotted two weathered bronzed feet appearing underneath her eyesight, toes dancing on the Persian rug. Each toe bore a faded tattooed number, from 1 to 10. The ink, far from fresh, had turned mossy and softened around the edge of the number. Clive bounced forward at her, his enthusiasm comical. He punctuated each word with a forward jump of his shoulders. 'Just peeking in to check on you, dear. Some of the girls said you had a few funny turns. That's no good, is it?'

'I think I should see someone. Is a doctor coming? The nurse? Is she back?'

Something, maybe irritation, flashed through Clive's wise face. The sinewy webbing between his fingers spoke of manual labour and extending himself in a way that just had to be self-flagellation. 'Yes, on their way, dear. In the meantime, feel free to nap. Perhaps one of the girls can get you something to eat or drink? A nibble, would suit you, yes?'

He poked his head outside. 'Everley, Abigail... could you, someone, grab Sophie some refreshments. Much obliged.'

Turning back to Sophie, he said 'I'll be sure to send the nurse in the second she gets back. Still delayed, I'm afraid.' He looked anything but regretful.

'Look, I think I really should go. I'll try and walk to my car and see my regular doctor.' The last few words came out in a mumble, her lips rolling across each other like slugs.

'You really shouldn't go anywhere.' He laid his hand on her arm which felt menacing but his cheerful smile counterbalanced it. His face held a glowing euphoria that looked a little like makeup. And whether it was her feeble mind acting up again, feeding her with the poison of paranoia, suddenly Sophie felt like she had to flee. Trying not to let her anxiety show, she struck back the heavy blankets that were pinning her to the uncomfortable makeshift bed. 'Actually, I need to go because I'm meeting someone this morning and they will be so confused about why I'm late!'

Clive's smile vanished as if Sophie had insulted him. He put his hand on her sternum and steadily pushed her back to laying down.

'No.'

It wasn't her mind tricking her. Sophie was in real trouble.

CHAPTER
TWENTY FIVE

Comfortingly mousey, Abigail gently pushed her way into the tent with a heavy book in her hand and a small, hand bashed copper bowl. Timidly, she approached Sophie and knelt beside her, her back as straight as it had been witnessing the sermon the night before.

'If you're about to read me passages of the fucking *Bible* you can fuck right off.' Sophie aimed at the woman.

'It's not *The Bible*,' she said softly.

'Unless it's a phone so I can call a doctor, you need to turn the fuck around and get out of these shambles of a freakshow camp and get me some help. My legs aren't working! I am too exhausted to move. Do you want to be responsible for this?'

'I bought you some food.' She carefully lay the bowl on Sophie's chest. The tang of orange segments sprinkled with tiny violets and rosemary sprigs sprang up at her. Unwilling to admit it, she was starving and incredibly thirsty.

After Abigail tenderly slid the segments into her mouth, Sophie decided to reason with her. 'Please. I think I'm going crazy. Having psychosis or something. Everything feels wrong. Can I see a doctor? Or speak to my therapist?'

'I'm sorry madame. That's not possible right now. But I want to assure you that everything is okay. You're going to be okay.' The earnestness in her eyes actually aggravated Sophie more than soothed her.

'That is absolutely not true. I need to take some Valium or something, my mind is going to split apart. I thought I heard a baby before!'

The woman hesitated and ran her fingers over the cover of the book. She opened it to a page, scanned it and looked back up at Sophie, her finger holding the place in the book. 'We don't have Valium here. I can get you a relaxing tea, a herb, if you like?'

'I don't want any tea from you whackjobs.'

The woman flinched. 'It's temporary.' She tugged her sleeves down and tucked her chin in. Her eyes darted to the opening of the tent and then back to Sophie.

'What?'

'It's temporary. The legs.'

'How do you know that?' Sophie hissed at her which made her recoil a little.

'It's in the tea.'

'Are you kidding me?' Sophie felt a rage that was new to her. All the anger that had been asleep inside her, from Alex leaving, from the resentment of having to go to therapy, from not being in the familiarity of her own home... all arose. 'You all ought to be arrested.'

'It's not what you think.' Abigail's face glumly fell.

'Well, what I think is that you've drugged and paralysed me and now you're keeping me hostage in the middle of...' Sophie gestured about the place with her screwed up face '...nowhere. And you're going to end up on the news and then in jail.'

'You did hear a baby,' she said quietly.

'There are babies here? That's inhumane.'

'Of course, there are babies here. They are so loved and taken care of more than anyone can believe. You, of all people, should see that.'

'Well if drugging someone is taking care of them, then you've got it twisted and the police should be called. The babies should be taken away. Where are their parents?' Sophie stared hard at Abigail, as if her eyes could coerce her into getting up, leaving the tent and sourcing help.

'I know where to find your husband.'

'I beg your fucking pardon? How do you know him? Where is he? Take me to him!' Sophie's eyes bulged. Her speech had become crystal clear with outrage.

'I can't... just please trust that this is all happening for good.'

Sophie reached toward her throat with a dense

arm. But as she connected with the woman's skin, she got an electric shock which made her pull back. 'I don't know! I don't know where he is exactly. I just wanted to give you some hope. I'm sorry, it was the wrong thing to say. I shouldn't have said anything.' The woman leant back a little from Sophie, her hands raised and fright on her face. She bowed her head lower so that Sophie could see her meticulous part, slicing from her forehead to the back of her head. 'Please,' she whispered, pushing her hands, which had sandwiched the book between them, towards Sophie.

Sophie slid it out and frisbeed it towards the tent wall. 'I told you that I don't want to read the fucking *Bible*,' she hissed at the woman, who looked horrified and scrambled after the book. She picked it up and smoothed its cover to make sure it was okay, hugging it back towards her chest like it was a kitten. Sophie's legs of lead were both a saviour and a frustration. If she were mobile, she would have held a lithe hand to Abigail's buttery neck and squeezed the sides, pressing on the tendons to make her squawk.

'I thought you would understand once you read it.' The woman's eyes and tip of her nose had reddened from crying. At that moment, Clive burst his way through the tent flaps and unflinchingly told the woman to get out. She obeyed, hanging her head even lower, dropping the book in front of her crotch. 'I'm so sorry, I just thought once she saw the book...'

'Get out.' Clive repeated stonily which left a motionless chill in the tent. He followed her out and Sophie sucked in so much air that her jaw strained and screamed and screamed for help, causing Clive to rush right back and bring his pointy nose up to her face.

'I want to get the fuck out of here Clive. Can't you see that? Can't you see that it's beyond insane to keep me here?'

'Insanity is... well a peculiar thing. As you know.'

'I don' know what you mean but I've had enough.'

'You've watched yourself go slowly insane recently. It's been like an unfurling that you cannot control. You cannot wind the thread back up inside itself once it has been snagged and left behind everywhere you tread. There's nothing or no one left that is safe to believe, especially not yourself. That must be... well, terrifying.' He gave a little shudder of glee when he said "terrifying".

'What the fuck do you know about all of this?' Sophie's wrath forced spittle out of her mouth and on to her chest. Just like the insanity that forced her to come undone, she could not control the fury that threatened to overpower her now. And what's more, is that she didn't care to. 'When I get out of here— and I will because how exactly do you think this will end?— you will be the first person I tell the police about and I will goad them into believing you did abhorrent things to me. And it will break you apart even more than I've been broken.' Sophie delivered her threat with an evenness that would have chilled even a long-serving school principal.

And then the anxiety came rushing up to her. The gritty feeling of yesterday that she had been introduced to since just before her thirtieth birthday. She felt like she had been washed in a wave of sand and prickles.

'Ahh yes, Alex. Where could he possibly be Sophie?' Sophie watched Clive's eyebrows sharpen into peaks.

'How do you know his name? Do you know my husband?' Sophie's imagination started unravelling and telling her things that she didn't want to hear. For better or worse, Clive obviously knew where Alex was. 'Where is he?' She screamed at him, pushing her elbows into the bed.

'Let's get very clear here Sophie, my dear. Nothing was happening when you were home, right? Alex wasn't coming back and you weren't even getting better?'

'Your fancy charlatan tricks may work with the rest of the fools here but I can smell your chicanery a mile off.'

Clive ignored her. 'In fact, if you take a look, an actual close look, weren't things getting objectively worse? The nightmares are increasing, you've lost your ability to trust your own judgement, you've been hearing things that are possibly not there. And then, just notice, where is Alex?' His hand fluttered across the air, like a stage magician.

Sophie gritted her teeth and roared at Clive's torment. The screams had left Sophie's ears ringing and her throat tingly but she could understand what he was saying. Again, she thought she heard the stifled cry of a baby but it could have easily been a magpie.

'No one can hear you out here. No one. So, stop screaming.' He sighed.

It wasn't until she heard herself say 'where is Alex?' again that she crumpled inside and the heat of grief burst through her stomach and chest. The unforgiving reality was nothing more than the fact that Alex, was indeed, not there. All the other was just irrelevant noise that Sophie had filled her head with to distract her from her Alex-less reality. The tent breathed with her. Closing in on her with every breath, as Clive and Sophie stared at each other wordlessly. Just then a tiny sparrow flew into the tent with purpose. It soared in a small circle, trying to find its way out but failed, knocking itself into the tent wall and falling to the ground. Flipping itself onto its feet, it shook its tiny head three times, so quickly that it looked like once, and hopped out through the small opening at the bottom of the door flaps. Sophie and Clive watched it, bemused by the absurdity of the timing.

'You know what that means, don't you Sophie?' Clive asked smugly. 'That means that a death is imminent.' He twirled on his heel and flicked his hand dismissively at her and stalked out of the tent.

CHAPTER TWENTY SIX

Sophie thought about the Wild Woman all afternoon as she lay uncomfortably in her tent, drifting into gossamer-thin sleep that stripped her of any rest. The chirping alarm of birds was a relief and pulled her out of the frightening visions of the Hecate like being that she imagined existed in the depths of either side of the woods.

Suddenly, two hands dove between the tent flaps and were followed by a mess of cocoa coloured hair. Curls that she knew too well and was never more glad to see.

'Carla! What are you doing here?'

'Hello, Sophie. Abigail thought perhaps I could help. I hear you're quite unwell. What are you doing here is the real question?'

Sophie was right. Carla did live nearby! 'Oh, Carla!

Thank you, thank you, thank you for coming to find me. You don't understand how relieved I am to see you. Please! You have to get me out of here. These people are full-blown nutjobs. And that's coming from someone on the brink of insanity. You have to get me out of here and I need to find Alex.'

'Okay, I can see that you're still back in this headspace of wanting to find Alex again. He left you Sophie and I think it's time you started to accept that.' Carla's eyebrows and mouth pulled away from each other.

Sophie was shocked. This was the first time that Carla had pulled her up on Alex leaving her. She had always remained impartial during their sessions, rarely passing opinion. 'Maybe we can talk more about that in our next session. Can you lift me? I can't walk. I think they've poisoned me.'

'It looks to me, that it's quite important that you need lots of rest Sophie. Do you agree?'

'Yes, I agree. I will do nothing but rest as soon as I get home. I see that is what I need now. And I'll even stop looking for Alex.' Sophie's neck twinged as she heard herself lie to the one person that she felt she could be honest to.

But as Carla gently nodded her head at Sophie, she felt like she was sinking further down a staircase, her shoulders forcing the rest of her body to the ground, her face sagging and her thoughts coming through slower, with longer gaps in between.

Sophie let tears worm out of her eyes. 'I'm so fucking tired Carla.'

'Yes, I see that.' Carla forgot herself for a moment and went to reach across to pat Sophie's head but hesitated and let her hand thump on the blanket. 'Okay, my best advice is to stay here for a little bit. You don't need to move just yet.' She looked at her delicate gold watch. 'I have... patients. I'll attend to them now and, in between, I'll arrange for a doctor or maybe an ambulance, to come and see you. Collect you perhaps. Hopefully, you'll be home in your own bed, resting, by dinner time.' Carla's smile lifted her cheeks and Sophie felt the same reassurance that she felt when she slid into her warm room for her sessions.

But she panicked, she didn't want to stay any longer than she had to, even if it was only an hour or two. 'Oh no, Carla please take me now. You must. Who knows what they will do to me here?'

'You're perfectly safe Sophie. I have known Clive for years and, although their methods seem a little... antiquated... they will look after you until I get someone to collect you.'

'Oh Carla, no. Please,' she begged pathetically.

'Enough,' Carla said sharply which cut off Sophie's wails. 'I simply cannot carry you and you might need medical attention.'

Carla was a good person. She was on her side. She was her therapist, for fuck's sake. Of course, she wasn't having an affair with Alex. Of course, she was only interested in helping Sophie get better and getting her back home. She probably had a duty of care that meant she wasn't even allowed to touch her patients. *I must have been so exhausted that my mind was playing absolute havoc on me! Carla isn't hiding Alex from me. The keyring is just a coincidence,* Sophie thought. She'd read about people who even only went two days without sleep and how they had such intense perceptual distortions that it changed them.

The cool relief ran through the blood of her arms. It was just her mind telling her stories because she was so tired. Bone tired. What else had she been telling herself about Alex? Sophie let her mind drift back to a foggy half memory of Alex's co-worker. How the work he'd been doing, coupled with some bullying from his boss, had stressed him out to the point where he decided to stay up most nights and keep working. After the fourth, or was it fifth— or did it even happen at all?— night his wife found him squatting over their toilet, his hand covered in creamy excrement as he tried to extract a robotic bug out of his arse. He had, somehow, cottoned on to the notion that aliens had implanted something into his anus and they were going to come back down to earth to collect him. He screamed at his wife that he had to get it out and flush it into the sewer system and that the '... bitch didn't understand and never understood him.' Sophie recalled the wife (did Alex tell her this or did she dream it?) saying that it wasn't even that he believed in aliens or the stress or delusions that had encouraged her to leave. It was just that she had seen his own shit on his hand that had so severely repulsed her that she couldn't evoke the initial love for him that she felt. Sophie squeezed her memories to recall where "shit hand guy" was now. *Didn't he recover and end up marrying someone he worked with? Or did he kill himself?* Perhaps this was all just an episode of *The X Files* that she once watched.

As she sorted and sifted through her memories and thoughts, putting them into neat little piles, she considered what she would do when she got home. Rest, as she had promised. Enough to get the strength to start searching for Alex again. But this time, she'll be more prepared. She'll eat more, maybe pack a bag and a spare phone. But as she waited and planned, the ambulance didn't come and neither did Carla.

CHAPTER
TWENTY SEVEN

E ven though her mind felt like it was holding its breath waiting for Carla to burst back through and take her home, she swore she could start to feel some small movement in her toes. Her legs were coming back to life! She waited a bit and then wiggled them again and it almost seemed like the blanket had rippled. Sophie decided to keep up the pretence that her legs weren't working for as long as she needed to, before she could surge free and run away if she needed to.

The hope she felt was enough for her to catch her breath and summon up a little energy. Carla would understand if she took off and didn't wait for her and she would be the first person she called when she got home safe, Sophie promised herself. Especially since Carla seemed to be taking her time. Perhaps the woods were harder to find from the road than Sophie originally thought. An ambulance van would have a hard time driving its way in here. Hopefully, the ambulance officers weren't on foot and lost.

Her planning and excitement were interrupted by guttural sounds. Like a koala's mating groan, throaty calls filled the evening. *Please, please don't let there be an orgy going on outside*, she begged to the air. That was more than she could bear. Even one of Clive's chintzy sermons would be more tolerable. But as she kept listening, she realised they were chanting. Some in unison, some in lag. The words she didn't recognise; it sounded like gibberish. Except there was one word she thought she might have recognised. *Veh-nusss. Veh-nusss.* It peppered their chants. She thought back to the Wild Woman Ceremony and rolled her eyes.

Despite the lulling rhythm of the chants, the way they mispronounced Venus really irked Sophie and she despised being stuck to the bed and inside the tent more than ever. Her frustrated wail brought in two of the women; ones she had not yet properly seen. They were indistinguishable from the rest. They, too, had the same fleecy jumpers and hair parted directly down the middle, a lack of colour, a lack of sprightliness about them that just made Sophie feel dusty inside. They were dull to look at. If they were a beverage, they'd be watery instant coffee. In the fading light, with the licks of firelight sneaking in behind them, they looked like bats. Their faces drawn long and comically menacing.

It was the only non-bland thing about them. Despite their scowling faces, they were excited. One woman gently bumped her palms together. 'It's time!'

'Time for what?' Sophie demanded.

'Venus time! It's here.'

The other woman stepped forward, right up to Sophie's side and started to slide her hand under her armpit.

'It's great! You'll see.' She hauled her upright and the other woman slid her arm underneath her knees. Together they awkwardly carried Sophie out into the night, outside of the tent. Sophie relaxed into their grip, letting herself sink. She was so delighted to be getting some fresh air, getting out of the miserly tent that she didn't even care what crackpot ritual or party was about to happen. Plus, she could see better if the ambulance was coming.

They positioned her on a wide rock in front of the fire, blankets still wound around her legs. Choosing to eat the rich potatoes that were doused in rosemary, sage and nettles— easing a weakness she attributed to lack of nourishment— she watched everyone around her tucking into the white fleshy globules, dribbles of bright yellow butter drip down their chins. If they were eating it, she was safe to do so. And she treasured the milky and fresh taste on her tongue and wanted more.

The chanting had ceased and a murmur of delinquent chatter spattered about the unformed circle.

Again, there was a palpable anticipation hovering and it was thrilling. Sophie caught the tail end of it. Through the wavy ether of the fire flames, she could see the men and women of the group differently to how they were. They were plumper, more jovial and spirited. Their clothes were of a by-gone era, a mixture of tatty items and far more formal and pristine numbers: a sharp vest here and a glinting monocle there. Around their feet scampered several small monkeys, also dressed partly in human attire. The women rushed in with widened hips and bottoms, enhanced by fabric and frames of clothing. Boots stomping and hands clapping, that added to the percussion of excitement. No matter how they looked, how they were dressed, they were all doing the same thing. Rubbing big oblong shapes over up and down their arms, over their necks, lifting the hem of their pants and skirts to rub up and down their shins and calves. They held these discs, which glinted warmly against the firelight, in their palms and raised them upwards, seemingly unwilling to pass to another. One woman had a pot full of old pennies that she passed out one coin at a time, jingling the pot in between each person. Everyone took their penny enthusiastically.

Everley emerged from the darkness between two of the medium-sized tents holding a peculiar box. The box looked like a handful of books squeezed together with button-sized satellite keys. Sophie thought she was holding an antique music box but when Everley started playing it like a squeeze-box, stretching and flexing the bellows to create and lengthen notes, it was obvious that it was an unusual musical instrument. She toggled at the keys with a deftness and sat down, resting the instrument on one thigh, all the while her mouth frozen in a half-smile. The sound was jarring but not altogether out of place as the scene before Sophie whirred and collided and confused her into losing her sense of reality. More than once, staring around at the people and fire before her, she forgot where she was and how she got there. Like a few times over the past few months, even before Alex left, her mind felt like it was melting and leant away from the fire, momentarily believing her brain was like a big goopy marshmallow that would threaten to melt out her eye sockets and ear holes.

Sophie thought about Alex, although he seemed to be fading in her mind: their days together, the joint activities, what he would wear on the weekends. A mental picture of his face was still there but some features shifted a little: she couldn't remember if he had a little curl of hair that kept flopping over his wide forehead or if she had imagined that. His earlobes were either really globular or pressed right to his skin, like they didn't exist at all. But Sophie discarded these particulars as irrelevant be-cause the feeling, the yearning, to find him and be with him again was still there. It wasn't question-able. If he were here, he would watch these people silently until the next day, when he would look at her earnestly and asking, straight-faced, 'it's Venus time!' and they'd guffaw at the shared joke all morning.

The chanting of 'Venus' returned and got more hurried and insistent and with each sibilation. Sophie felt like she had been flung around a merry go round, her eyes watering from dizziness. None of the faces that surrounded her were particularly interested in Sophie and she didn't know who to screech out for to stop her from tumbling over and over, so she held her breath and waited for the vertigo to be over. Surprising herself, she longed to be back in the small tent in the safety of her narrow hard bed.

The people around the fire came to a hush as Clive, grinning so hard that his face looked like it couldn't stand up to it anymore, bounced through, gesturing for everyone to quieten down with his arms. 'Venus is!' He bellowed to the fire circle and everyone cheered untidily. 'Alright, alright. Shhh.' Clive pointedly looked everyone in the eye, lingering on Sophie. There was an incomplete silence. Cracks of the fire danced around them, a very faint bleating of a sheep and the shuffling of feet on dirt. Clive held them in that state of taciturnity until it was awkward and it made Sophie want to scream but instead, she sniffed and made herself promises that she would do what it takes to get away from this group the second even one of her legs came back to life. She ached to wiggle her toes to see how it was progressing but didn't dare in case someone saw. Waiting until she was put back in the tent and everyone was asleep was her only option.

The silence became even more uncomfortable, which Clive derived drips of glee from, like a grapefruit being squeezed into his mouth. He clapped his hands sharply three times and then he began. 'Finally. Finally!' He shouted with so much intensity that a few people noticeably jumped. 'We have been waiting for this moment for decades, some of us, nay all of us, for lifetimes. Ever since our first Senior opened up about The New Way to accept the power of Venus and all its alchemical gifts and bringings, we have awaited this. And through the Universe's willing, not to discount the hard work of all of us...' he paused to nod at a few people around the circle, '... we are closer than we have ever been to accepting our birthright and mission in harnessing the alchemical controls that reside in all of us but for those who choose not to see. Every one of you has chosen not to live in the dark anymore. You have chosen to be the people to truly see. To stop the limiting notions that have been imposed on us as humans for centuries. To only accept what we have been told we can do, is in our capacity. But not you, no you have accepted a higher way. A lighter way. And, we can all agree, a better way!'

A collection of applause punctuated his sentiments. Sophie could barely swallow back down all the hot bile that was rising. Looking around the campfire again, all traces of how she saw them had transformed. There they were, all wearing their white jumpers like they had always been. No out-dated costumes, no squeezebox, no monkeys. A trick of the fire mirage.

'After many attempts that have all lit up the cor-rect, and proper, pathway but have not seen us share this moment, until now, we can all rejoice in the fact that our efforts are finally being paid off in the most exquisite and rewarding of ways. And that the seed of Venus is now finally with us, after our years of searching and spellwork and sum-moning. The seed is here.' Again, more applause and cheers. The two men had clamped a hand each on the other's shoulder, in triumphant comradery. Sophie felt her throat harden and watched the faces of those around her. They were all eating it up like he was dishing out bowls of chocolate and they were starving. Everything that he said was a bunch of nothing meaning words. But if they meant nothing, why was Sophie uncurling inside herself? She longed for one of her fainting spells, induced or not, so she didn't have to bear witness to this derangement.

Emerging from the trees, came the billowing curls of Carla. Sophie almost squealed and knew that her willingness to escape had brought her rescuer in the form of the very person that had been rescuing her from herself all along. But the unhurried way that Carla moved forward unnerved Sophie more than she already was. She searched for her silky eyes but they had turned beady and focused and they all but swept past Sophie without recognition, like a laser scanner looking for something to identify.

'Carla, help me. They won't let me go!' Sophie strangled out a plea.

Carla contemplated Sophie for a second, with a sideways tilt of her angular chin and squinted her eyes at her with a pity that could have blown apart the circle of campers. Sophie slumped forward as soon as she realised Carla was wearing one of the signature jumpers with a big "X" painted on the front. Everley placed a delicate hand on Sophie's back and was making half-hearted circles which she didn't have the energy to shrug off. Who was this woman that she had split herself open for and shared all of her most disturbing experiences and fears with? Clive answered her question with more of a bounce and wobble on his toes. 'Our valiant leader is here, everybody!' Sophie blocked her ears to more sickening applause.

'Enough!' Carla shrieked so loudly and sharply that even Sophie could hear it through her plugged ears. Everything went ghastly still. Even the fire seemed to cower in response. 'This will not come as welcomed news. Yes, we have reached a stage we have been awaiting for nearly thirty years but I have to inform you that more testing is required.'

Sophie watched as a few people around the circle flopped forward, dismayed. Despite Abigail weeping into her hands, Sophie still couldn't understand what was really happening and she felt so very on the outer, which pressed her to want to escape even more. To forget about this place and its weird antiquated people like it was a fever dream. Sophie tried to subtly turn around and scan the clearing for the best escape route. But Everley, who was still rubbing her back, mistook the action and leant in to hug her, obscuring her view past the group. The distant baby wail floated in briefly again and upon hearing it, she really did start to believe she was in one of her lengthy nightmares.

'Bring her out!' Carla shouted back to the tents. By now, she stood upon a wooden crate that had been covered in a small crocheted blanket of orange and reds, which mirrored back the fire. The light from the fire was throwing shadows on Carla's face that distorted the woman that Sophie knew. Her nose edged forward more and her eyes were sharper, a harder, more sinister look had emerged and Sophie missed the soft, warm woman that had taken all her vulnerabilities and wrapped them up for her.

Clive leapt up to Carla and tugged at her forearm. 'Are you sure...?' He tried to postulate but Carla shook him off roughly and he stumbled back, falling on his backside. It was only when Sophie noticed that rather than embarrassment, Clive showed a concern that distorted his face, so he looked like a child and an old man, all at once.

A woman rushed forth from the biggest tent, her arms out in front of her carrying another bundle of crocheted blankets with more muted colours of flamingo and fairy floss pinks. A wail erupted through the navy-blue night and Sophie could feel the surrounding trees lean in protectively. The sound made her look up towards the rich blanket that held them all steady, the decorated night sky that offered both freedom and containment. The sky pulsed and loomed closer, begging Sophie for something that she could not translate. Carla held the baby up in her hands, cradling its head and rear in each hand. The crocheted blanket fell to the floor and the baby's mouth screamed open so wide it almost took over its tiny head. Sophie heard Abigail gasp and start to sob to match the baby's wail.

'Abigail, since you seem so upset, this test will be good for you to conduct. Will you step forward please Abigail?' Abigail shook her head into her hands, her pitted sobs continued.

'Abigail. Consider yourself on the other side of this. The growth, the revitalisation and the empowerment. You can reach your potentiality by seeing through this task and you know it. Otherwise, you can stay stagnant in your resistance and probably keep butting up against whatever inner turmoil this is causing you again and again until you learn this precious lesson. You have a choice.' The choice that Carla presented was barely so. Sophie didn't really comprehend what Carla was proposing but Abigail dug her toes into the dirt and her sobs had morphed into a funnelled yowling.

'Abigail? Would you like to come forward?' She shouted over the baby's cries which had syncopated with Abigail's.

Everley had moved over and crouched beside Abigail. She scooped her hands under one elbow and coaxed her up. Abigail resisted but not enough. She was led to where Carla was standing, presenting the baby to Abigail to take hold. Carla slid the baby into Abigail's arms where she hunched over the bright red thing, sobbing into its face. Her hair hung like a shield between the baby and the onlookers and Sophie watched her shoulders jiggle up and down because she couldn't see her face or the baby and she couldn't predict what was going to happen. But the way that her stomach had crimped itself, like the end of a toothpaste tube being squeezed, ensured that what was about to happen was going to be horrific.

'You have a choice, Abigail. Continue as you have been or push yourself to new echelons. Release yourself from your poisoned narrative and break free to be the limitless being that you can be. For once you hit that space, you will be helping your fellows to get there also. And collectively, we are going somewhere great. Somewhere that humans have always been calibrated to be. Do it now Abigail!' Carla was screeching but at the sky, rather than at Abigail. Her cheeks shot around like a rabid dog, like they had been hit with a Newton's Cradle. 'I can't! I can't!' Abigail tried to hand the baby, who had sensed its need to be quiet and subdued as a matter of survival, back to Carla. But she was rebuffed by Carla's outstretched palms.

'Abigail. You know that's not the best choice for the highest good of you and your fellows now, do you?' Carla's voice became nastily sing-songy.

'But I don't want to do this! I don't care about growth anymore. I'm obviously not made for this kind of evolution!'

Sophie watched Abigail transform from a virtuous and meek maiden to a venomous rat. And her rage was contagious and it was hard not to root for her. Carla snatched the baby back and stepped off the box. She leaned her face in close to Abigail, who had stopped crying but her cheeks were still shiny from the tears. 'I want you to do something, Abigail.' Carla's voice had floated to a level and calm tone.

'Yes, Carla?' Abigail resigned herself to a final sniffle and looked at her feet.

'I want you to get the fuck out of my sight!'

Abigail scampered off to a tent that Sophie couldn't see and she let out the breath that she'd been holding. A few others around her did the same.

The whole time, Clive didn't remove his eyes from Carla's face, nodding in agreement with whatever she said. Turning back to face her mignons, Carla looked each in the eye, daring a defiance that she could unleash her unsettled rage upon, now that the dragon inside her had been stirred awake. 'You all make me sick,' she spat and then turned to nod at Clive, who was caked in adoration at her side. He reciprocated the firm nod and slowly made his way around the circle, gently landing a hand on each shoulder, smiling as if he'd just been told the secret of life. No one flinched or tensed under his touch and Sophie wondered if she would be patted the same since, essentially, she was an outsider. But when he came to her spot, he moved in front of her and yanked her forearm so hard that Sophie felt a twinge in its socket. Clive gripped her arm tightly and yanked her towards the fire. They were at the fire's edge before Sophie recovered from the momentary shock and realised what was about to happen. The warmth on her face peeled her eyes open and washed away the grogginess, yet her legs stilled remained comatose, so Clive had to drag her, the side of her hip grinding on the dirt. Sophie screamed and contorted herself away from his hand but it was futile without the use of her legs. Clive plunged her forearm into the fire and the pain radiated up through Sophie's chest and cheeks and rendered her silent. She felt as if her lungs had emptied themselves never to stretch to fullness again and her voice box had withered in an instant. She couldn't see, her blindness was fuelled by searing agony.

Clive pulled back her arm and discarded it aside in the dirt, leaving Sophie gasping for air, her lips pressed into the dirt and bark, uncaring what fell into her mouth. As she ebbed in and out of fainting, Sophie tried hard to stay awake and keep her eyes on something around her, purely for survival. Confusion swam at her and it appeared as if the whole place was lit up, like a UFO had targeted the spot and washed everything in its white light. She could see everyone's face under the white light but she didn't remember even turning her head to look. She could still taste the dirt. Every inhale stuffed her nostrils with more and more sand. There was a flash of white and then the feeling drained from her arm and she, once again, surrendered to darkness.

CHAPTER TWENTY EIGHT

Sophie awoke in the dark, back in the tent on the unforgiving bed. A headache held her hostage and her teeth chattered like a battered typewriter. Each chatter hurt her wincing jaw and rattled her eyeballs, feeling gritty against an invisible sandpit. She peeled her eyelids apart and scanned the interior of the tent where she lay. The small movement of scanning the room made her whole body shudder with pain. It felt as if she was locked in a suit of iron that was clamping down and tightening on her. As the tent flaps opened she was reminded about the bright flash and the torture of having her arm burnt. 'My arm,' Sophie tried to whisper at Everley, who ushered in cradling a basket of items.

'It's just temporary. I'll attend to it,' and methodically she unpacked the items from the basket: a small jar, some bandages, a bottle of yellow liquid, a small bottle of Whisky and a small tinder box. Everley sighed and placed her hands on the bed, looking up at Sophie after she had lined all her bottles up. 'Sophie, this is going to be unpleasant but I promise you, with all that I can promise you, that you will feel miraculous for it.'

Sophie willed an ounce of relief out of Everley but it didn't come. 'What exactly are you going to do? And, once again, for the hundredth time, shouldn't you be getting me a doctor? Your backyard witchery shit is not going to even dent the crime, because that's what it is, I'll remind you. A crime that you all committed as you stood on and watched!'

'Please settle down. There's no point getting yourself into a state. There is more at play here than you can see from your vantage point. And in time, it will all make sense.'

'If there's ever a time where someone grabbing my arm and shoving it into a fire to give me third-degree burns makes sense to me, I should have my head read.' Pain stopped her from spewing any more anger as Everley grabbed at her burnt arm. Sourness forced its way up to her mouth and she opened it, salivating wildly down her face. Her eyes burned with tears and she searched for Everley's eyes, hoping if she could witness Sophie's tremendous pain, that she would somehow realise how much trouble she was in and seek medical help.

Everley held her gaze like she was watching a road,

her eyelids dropping in heavy, unfazed blinks. Everley pulled back Sophie's blankets and she felt the cool air swim around her chest, as she tried to look down at herself to see she had no top on. But really, she was angling for a view of her arm. She couldn't imagine what it looked like as she'd never seen a severe burn. The pain was so great, so intense and nullifying that she wasn't even sure that she still had an arm attached and she refused to move her fingers to test.

'Righto, drink this.' Everley held out the whiskey bottle to Sophie, whilst keeping her eyes on the injury. Sophie clutched at the bottle with her working arm, which was half trapped underneath her torso and pushed her mouth towards it. Gasping, she gurgled as much back as she could before her throat begged for a break. She felt drips of whiskey hit her chin and chest and wished she could lick them off herself as if they were the answer to all the pain relief left in the world.

'Alright, settle down,' Everley yanked back the bottle, not letting Sophie finish it. 'And here, drink this also.' She lifted an old milk bottle filled with syrupy blonde liquid, which slanted in the neck of the bottle with each movement.

'What is it?' Sophie could smell something rancid escaping from the neck of the bottle; like sour milk and metal.

Everley looked like she was already fed up with Sophie and the treatment had not even begun. She hit a sigh hard. 'It's a remedy we make. It will numb your body and will dull the pain enough for you to get back to your senses.'

'What's in it? Just give me more whiskey. And surely you have some fucking codeine or something?' The alcohol had eased her headache and sent the slightest buzz through her skin but with the courageousness of whiskey Sophie's voice catapulted a little louder.

'Honestly, this stuff is better than codeine or booze. Really, I don't care if you don't have it but you best stay still when I apply the treatment,' Everley said pointedly.

'Bullshit! What treatment do you think you're putting on my arm? You should be getting me to a burns unit!'

'Sophie. Relax. The treatment will have your arm repaired by the time you wake up tomorrow. That is not an exaggeration. My advice, because I actually know what I'm doing, believe it or not, is to drink some of the elixir and shut up. And then I'll give you more whiskey.'

Sophie, without much to lose, was frantic for more whiskey to help ease the dazzling agony that shot from her elbow to the centre of her chest. 'Fine. But please assure me that this isn't poisonous and won't kill me?'

'It's not going to do either of those things. You've had it before anyway. You just didn't know it.'

'Is this the shit that's been put in my tea that has paralysed me?'

'Yes. A modification of, anyway. This is a special

batch that is made for strong pain relief. It works. Trust me.'

'Why in the fuck would I trust a snake like you? You're all a bunch of poisoners!' Sophie spat at her. Everley went to grab Sophie's arm to squeeze a little more sense into her but she stopped. Yanking her sleeve toward her elbow, she shoved the underside of her arm a few inches from Sophie's face. 'There. That's why you should trust me. You want the pain gone? Drink it. You want it healed quicker than you can believe? Let me do my thing.'

Sophie looked at the bubbled lilac flesh where Everley had been burned. It had puckered into a small circle and lacked the anger that should have been there. 'Will I get paralysed?'

'Yes. For a short time. It wears off after a few days. Sophie, we're definitely not going to kill you if that's what you're worried about. You're far too valuable to us. You'll see.'

'I don't know what any of that means but I really, really just want the pain to end now.'

'Good girl.' Everley lifted the bottle of yellow goop to her mouth and started to pour, Sophie took a tiny sip that barely covered her tongue and waited. 'You'll need a little more than that. Have three big gulps and wait.' Sophie followed her instructions nervously and shut her eyes tight and waited, praying to nothing that she would be okay and that someone would find her soon.

Before she even finished her prayer, her body started to slacken and her mouth lost its grip. Like being washed in the shallows, the pain, the muscle tension, the headache... it all just left her body and was superseded with relief. The agony had been so damming that the reprieve was as sweet as the morning sun. Endorphins shot through her, making her feel invincible. Until she remembered that she couldn't move anything but her head. She tried to mumble something at Everley but her lips were wonky so she gave in to the sweet freedom while Everley worked away at her arm, concentrating hard and carefully selecting items from her basket.

CHAPTER
TWENTY NINE

S ophie slept through the night like she was on a tropical paradise vacation and all the stress had left her body. When she awoke the next morning, she held her breath as she waited for the pain to rush back in.

But the pain never came. She could move her arms slightly, even with stilted joints. Her legs, however, were as lifeless as the dead birds by the door that awaited Sophie back at her home. She jiggled out of the blankets, eager to look at her injury. The blanket fell away and she looked at both arms with confusion. Her injured forearm was covered in a slimy clear film, shining like plastic. And underneath was the tiniest small star-shaped etching, the size of a gumnut. It was pink, like the raw skin of a dog nose. But there was no anger to it. No trauma, no peeling flesh. Barely any hint of burn at all. Whatever Everley had done, had worked. It had worked so well, in fact, that Sophie doubted she was even awake and stuck in some kind of bliss dream that would end all too soon. She summoned her limp fingers to pinch at her face to wake her from her spell but they did nothing but grab at her grimy face and slip off. Sophie felt her fingers on her cheek like she did any other day.

Someone had put a jumper on her and she looked to the ground to see the bottle of whiskey empty, tipped over, the neck hovering over a dark wet patch.

As she was scanning the ground, Everley appeared. 'You're awake. How's the arm?'

'It's… fine actually. How did you do that?'

'We have our ways.'

'What happened to Abigail? Can you send her in to me?' Sophie was more troubled by the Abigail disturbance than her own incident.

'Abigail is being punished. As she should be,' Everley rolled her eyes.

'Punished for what?'

'You saw that pitiful display last night. She's barely one of us. Show me your arm.' Everley cuffed Sophie's wrist with her thumb and forefinger and slid it towards her. 'Well. That has cleared up astoundingly well, wouldn't you say so? No pain, I'm assuming.' She cocked an eyebrow at Sophie.

'No pain,' she said reluctantly.

Everley went and collected Clive to show him her handiwork and together they inspected the small remnants of the burn. 'Now, Sophie, you simply must forgive me for my actions. It may have seemed cruel, I know, but it was a necessary part of a bigger picture. Of a test that we all must go through. You especially,' Clive stretched his trademark smile at her.

Sophie spat in his face. Nonchalantly, he wiped his face and continued to smile. 'Has it not healed spectacularly? We needed to do this Sophie. It's part of a process.'

'What process? Keeping me here, drugging me and burning me is not some process. It's a series of crimes that you need to wake up from your delusion about and get me the fuck out of here.'

'Oh contraire, Sophie. You trespassed on private property, quite inebriated one might add, and must have somehow fallen into an open fire stumbling around. You're lucky you didn't get mistaken for a wild animal that could be shot.' And through all the smiles, the warmth and the welcoming act that Clive had been committed to since Sophie met him, his poisonous insides mushroomed. Despite his stuck grin, Sophie could see the flecks of gold in his eyes were never there, they were flecks of snake scales. With all her reserves, Sophie reigned herself in and set her face serenely as possible. 'Look, I'm really not interested in getting you in trouble. I'm just looking for my husband. You have my word that if you take me home, I'll never utter a word of this place to anyone. Least not the police.' Sophie pressed her lips together and nodded, in what she hoped was an earnest display of truth. He laughed venomously and left her alone in her tent.

A short time later, amid Sophie's pangs of hunger and as her head whirred over what had happened, Clive shuffled inside the tent and looked at Sophie sheepishly. He hung his head, grasping one wrist with his other hand and wiped the top of his bare foot with the other in nervousness. 'Listen Soph, our angel, I want to apologise. I haven't been acting right towards you. I've meditated over it and I came to see that I was letting my worry about you and distress over your own anguish come out as anger, as pettiness. I want you to know that I've atoned and I will no longer be treating you this way. You don't deserve it and it really has nothing to do with you. I especially want you to know that you are most welcome here. I hope you'll forgive me.' He hung his head even lower waiting for a response.

'What is this atoning that you have done?' The power had shifted and Sophie felt like she was about to gain back some control.

'The punishment is decided by the Tarot. I was dealt the ten of cups so I drank ten cups of copper water.'

'Excuse me, the Tarot? As in playing cards? They decide how you make up for something? How does a little bit of cardboard dictate how you make up for poisoning and burning someone?'

'I know it may sound absurd to a newcomer but we have much trust in mystical ways and the Tarot does not let us down. If you see that there's a better fitting punishment for the way I have treated you I will accept it now.'

Sophie scanned her mind for something to torture him with. Surely, she could summon something better than a pack of cards could. 'Simple. Let me go.'

'That is out of my control. A more personal punishment, perhaps?'

'Curious, what would happen if you drew a pentacles card?'

'Give away my money.'

'I see. And wands?'

'A spell would be cast upon me.' Clive looked worried.

'Swords?'

'Stabbed,' he mumbled at her.

'I'd say you got off lightly then, didn't you?' Sophie was relishing in the new change of power dynamic. Did she have it in her to order him to be stabbed? Would she have to do the stabbing? Could she?

Sophie watched as Clive's legs wobbled and he crumpled to his knees.

'Please. Do not humiliate me any further. You think I am not humiliated enough living an existence that is unconventional? You think I don't feel like an idiot standing up in front of people and channelling a voice from another planet? On paper that's textbook lunacy. You think I didn't want for a life where I was happy being an accountant in my one-bedroom home, saving most of my wage for children that I would never have? Well, strangely I did. I was oddly content. And many parts of me still wish to this day that I could go back to that life now and be just as content. I did not choose to follow this path and accept these beliefs; they were part of my DNA before I was ever born and fighting them are futile.

No one, outside of this group, applauds you for following the unbeaten track. The rewards that we flog ourselves for daily are not seen in our everyday lives. We do not have yearly family vacations to celebrate all our hard work. Our rewards come at the end. Perhaps near, although we have no real way of knowing, outside of gut feelings and our faith. If you seek to humiliate me then please know that it has already been done enough for three lifetimes and your efforts will be in vain.'

Sophie could tell that he was right. Not knowing if it was her utter exhaustion or Clive's impassioned declaration and the first time she had seen him truly vulnerable, something within her softened. Seeing him weakened to his knees made her choke on pity and when pity rushes in, there is no room for anger. She found herself saying. 'I just don't understand why you act like you hate me? I don't want to be here anymore than you want me here. And yet, it seems as though you won't help me to get back home?'

'I know, I know it seems that way!' He pleaded with her, grabbing her hand and pressing it to his forehead, like she was some Ancient Egyptian goddess. 'But believe me, we're just trying to make sure you are okay and healthy. We don't have a car to transport you back to the city and we can't risk you going to hospital or the police with traces of our special tea in your blood. It should be gone by tomorrow and then, I promise, we will walk you to the road and help you get a lift back home. I promise Sophie.' He lifted his eyes which had changed to the colour of cinnamon donuts and stared at her. She watched his eyelashes dart up and down for a bit while she thought.

'I want to go home, Clive. I have no interest in going to a hospital really. They will likely section me and I just don't think I need that right now. It will make me worse and it will prevent me from searching for Alex.'

'Good, good,' he nodded with relief. He stood up to leave but as an afterthought, he turned back to her, 'Sophie, do you think that since you have been here, you've been feeling... better?' He pointed to his head as he said this.

'Well, no obviously I've been feeling quite paralysed and exhausted since I've been here!' She set herself up to start yelling at him but she remembered his promise that he would help her get home tomorrow. Something else started to dawn on her. He was right. Her mind was much better since she had happened upon the camp. And she hadn't had the nightmare once.

CHAPTER THIRTY

Sophie awoke and even though she lifted her eyelids, everything stayed the same hopeless black. But she forgot herself and went to swing her legs out from under the covers and was delighted to discover they moved somewhat. Barely able to feel her feet, they were numb as they hit the floor. But she forced weight upon them and found herself able to perform an awkward crawl, using her hands on the ground.

Carefully, she snuck out of her tent, peeling back the flaps bit by bit, afraid of what might wait for her on the other side. But the only sign of life outside was the fire which had dropped smaller into a bundle of neon red coals, casting an eerie glow on the ground around it. The red made Sophie think of an 80s nostalgia movie, all stereotypical horror and cliché. She almost laughed at the irony.

Scanning the empty seats that rimmed the fire and the motionless tents, Sophie tried to get her bearings to scramble her way out, back down the hill to the road. She no longer wanted to wait to see if Clive would keep his promise. Although she was sure she had come in from one way, everything seemed flipped around. And in the dark, she couldn't tell where the land rose and where it fell. But she didn't care, she was desperate and would rather spend the night in the middle of isolated scrublands, without even the birds for company, than be kept a prisoner of the unhinged people of the camp in their matching jumpers. Limping, with her hands pressed to the ground, she shot off towards a wall of darkness, widening her eyes so she would see whatever she was about to run into. Her shoulder bumped a tree and she resisted the urge to cry out.

Rising and falling voices made her stop dead. Both quiet and angry. It was hard to tell but she thought they were coming her way. Clinging to the tree, she held her breath and turned her ear towards the voices to work out if they were coming closer or veering off. It was unmistakably Clive and Carla, arguing with muted volume. Lightly suppressed rage in Carla's voice and confusion and pleading in Clive's. Sophie could only garner scraps of conversation but they argued as if they were lovers. Sophie still couldn't tell if they were moving or staying still. They could have been a mere four metres away; it was hard to tell without the advantage of sight.

'We have to do it now. There's no point in putting it off any longer,' Clive begged.

'I'm telling you, she is not ready. I've been probing her every session that we've had and she is clueless.'

'That doesn't mean that we can't do it.'

'It absolutely means we cannot do it. It means that it didn't work at all or, worse, we've got the wrong person.'

The silence after Carla's declaration stretched through the air like a thick rubber band. And Sophie gulped as she realised who they were talking about. *What are they going to do to me?* Sophie screamed internally.

'What about her nightmares?' Clive asked hopefully.

My nightmares, Sophie thought. *Why do they want to know about them?*

'There are those. They are a fair indication that she is the right one. Unless it's a wild coincidence and, look, stranger things have happened. As we know.'

'Well, surely we have to try? It's been such a long time coming.'

'Fine. Let me think about it. I mean, we can't very well let her go alive now, can we?'

Sophie heard Clive sigh so loudly and despondently that it shocked her out of her eavesdropping. An icy chill, like a caterpillar crawling up her spine, hit her as she felt them coming closer. They were planning to kill her.

Still on all fours, she scrambled away and found herself at the opening of the big shed. A light ringed the entrance, so she continued her awkward crawl towards it. The pain relief concoction had mostly worn off the top half of her body, she realised, as the palms of her hands retracted into themselves with every sharp rock underneath. Slowly pulling the door towards her, she was relieved to hear that it didn't squeak. Pushing a shoulder through, she lay her torso across the doorway, searching for whoever was inside. But it was empty of people.

Once inside, she combed the entire shed for any kind of vehicle or weapon, she would have even been grateful for a bicycle at that point. But what she saw inside, under the dull light of hurricane lamps, was just the rows and rows of amber jars, atop chocolate wood shelving and grated metal steps that housed even bigger jars, caramel coloured ceramic canisters, blue glass bottles and small wooden boxes and larger wooden crates filled with dried and fresh herbs. Interspersed throughout the containers were chunks of peacock green rocks. The burnt wreath and table had been removed since the dinner but the same smell waited. There were coils of copper wire stocked up behind a small canning machine and a kiln as well as a stripy bag filled with the horrible jumpers that everyone wore. More heaped piles of the same rocks were in almost every corner.

Sophie noticed more things that weren't obvious during the dinner party. Earth coloured pottery filled her eyeline and a handful of torso sized ceramic tanks were lined up like people. Each with a single symbol drawn on them in marker. And behind those tanks was a shelf as long as a car. It was hard to see, almost invisible against the shed wall, but Sophie spotted what the shelf was boasting: a row of books, all the same in their brown skins, pressed against one another. The same book that Sophie was drawn to in Carla's office. The same book that Abigail carried with her that she mistakenly thought was *The Bible*.

Stretching over the top of the tanks, Sophie slid one of the books off the shelf and into her hand, tucking it into the waistband of her pants. Now that feeling was beginning to slowly return to the lower half of her body, she felt the book's coolness press on her. The buzz it gave her washed away the fugue that she had been drowning in. *Evidence*, she thought as she tapped the book through her clothes.

'What are you doing?' A mouse whisper blew in behind her.

Sophie turned around to see Abigail looking at her, her eyes shiny and wide with concern.

'Oh Abigail... ' Sophie clasped Abigail's wrist and she angrily shook it free.

'You're not allowed to be in here.'

'Oh, aren't I?' Sophie feigned her dumbness.

'I'm going to get Clive.'

'No, Abigail, please don't do that. Please. Let's just talk a bit?' Sophie had no idea how she was going to get away from Abigail but she felt compelled to talk to her, connect with her. The way she reacted to the big fire told Sophie that Abigail wasn't really like the rest of them. Maybe she had been kept here against her will too.

'I'm already in so much trouble with the others.' As Abigail swung her face more into the light, Sophie noticed she was paler and her eyes had sunken, as if they were retreating from the horror that she saw.

'You shouldn't be in trouble Abigail! You've done nothing wrong. Can't you see that?'

'Oh, but I have! The rules of living here, under Venus, is that I must not disrespect the leader and I must do as they wish. Plus, I failed the trial.'

'When you ran away, they ended up burning me. But you weren't to know, Abigail.' Sophie threw in a little bit of guilt to knock Abigail's sensibilities about. The innocence of the young girl was almost unbearable to witness. It must be hell for her to live, especially in a camp that is governed by weird rules and rituals.

'Abigail, what did they want you to do to that baby?'

She pressed her lips together and inhaled, silent tears already dripping down her cheeks.

'You can tell me, Abigail. I'm not going to judge you. In fact, you're the only one here that I trust. I've wanted to be friends with you since the moment I met you.'

Abigail dipped her chin lower and nodded.

'Tell me.' Sophie slowly reached her outstretched palm out to land on Abigail's arm. This time she let it stay.

'They wanted me to...' She shook her head, looking at her feet, overcome with emotion. 'It's part of the heat initiation ritual, you see.'

'Did they want you to hurt the baby?'

'They wanted me to do what happened to you with the fire.'

Sophie couldn't help herself, she threw her hands to her mouth and stared at Abigail in horror.

Immediately defensive, she lifted her chin and sniffed her tears away. 'I wasn't going to do it! And anyway, just like you, it heals quickly.'

'Oh, Abigail. They should never have asked you to do that. That's abuse, can't you see that?'

'You don't understand. You don't know what it's all for. Even though you should.'

'What do you mean?'

'Nothing. Forget it. You haven't grown up here like I have.'

'Have you been in this camp since you were a kid?'

'Since I was born, yes.'

It was then that Sophie realised that Abigail was a lot younger than she had first noticed, which explained her fragility and the yearning that had been growing inside of Sophie to take care of her.

'Where are your parents?'

Abigail shrugged and said, 'People here are my parents. They are my family.'

Sophie felt a pang; they were both parentless daughters. 'Have you ever been outside the camp? Into the city?'

'A few times. Briefly. I didn't like it. It was noisy and brash. Full of heathens.'

'Oh, sweetheart. That doesn't mean you should have to stay here. Especially, when they are forcing abuse on you.'

'I have nowhere else to go. There's no other way I know how to live.'

Sophie made a rapid, dangerous decision at that moment. 'Come with me. I'm going to leave and go back home. You can stay with me and I will keep you safe.'

Abigail looked dubious and Sophie instantly knew she said the wrong thing.

'I ca-ca-can't do that. You can't do that.'

Sophie felt like an idiot. Of course, she wouldn't leave her family and the only life she had ever known for a stranger. And she'd just revealed her attempt to leave.

'Look forget I said that. I'm just going to go back to my tent now and get some sleep. I don't need to leave, really. But you know what it's like to be in trouble with Clive and Carla and I really don't want to agitate them any more than I have, since I'm new here and all. Could we make a deal to keep this meeting just between us? And I won't tell them what you've said to me?'

Abigail looked at Sophie with hesitation. 'Fine.'

Sophie slipped out the door she came, leaving Abigail to contemplate the interaction. As she stepped backwards out into the night, she watched Abigail's face as she realised there was a hole on the shelf of books.

CHAPTER
THIRTY ONE

S ophie barely made it more than a few steps
when she heard a wail that seemed to lift the
shed up from the ground. 'Shit. Abigail!' Sophie screamed back at the shed. But it was too late.
Two sets of vice-like hands encircled her arms. The
lacey floral smell of Carla eddied around her. Clive
yanked her other arm forward, his hands smaller
than Carla's but just as unforgiving. 'Carla please!'
Sophie begged and let her legs go limp and drag
along the ground. Carla remained stoically silent
whilst Clive kept glancing at her for instructions.
They dragged her back into the shed, kicking her
legs to get her over the threshold of the door and
discarding her on the floor. Whilst Clive held her
down, Sophie wriggled and aimlessly punched at
them, which had no effect. Carla looked up and saw
Abigail, who had turned grey watching the scene

unfold.

'Figures,' Carla sneered. 'Clive,' she summoned.

The leaders left the shed together, Sophie trying desperately to scramble after them but her heavy legs wouldn't hurtle her in time before the door slammed shut with a tinging sound. Elbowing at the door, Sophie knew that it was locked and her efforts futile. A quick scan of the shed told her there were no other escape routes and she locked eyes on Abigail who had melted to her knees, crying silently. 'I'm so sorry Sophie. I didn't know they would lock us in here.'

Sophie slumped down at the shed's door. And for the first time since she arrived at the camp, felt utterly helpless. The defeat of being at the mercy of others was compounded by the fragile sparrow of a girl before her. Which, despite raising alarm and getting her trapped in here, she felt sorry for.

Sophie crawled over to Abigail and put her arms around her, which only served to make Abigail weep more. Her nurturing instinct took over and she swept part of her straw-coloured hair back from her temple and whispered that everything was going to be alright. 'They're not going to keep you in here for long. You're one of them!'

'I'm not really. I never live up to their expectations. I'm weak.'

Sophie searched for something more reassuring to say. 'You know, even if they keep us in here, my husband would surely be looking for me by now and you just never know. The police are bound to find my car.' Sophie didn't believe any of what she was saying, especially the part about her husband. There was no way that Alex would be looking for her or even have noticed that her desperate communication had petered off. Especially if he had found the arms of another, which was as clear as day now, definitely not Carla.

It worked though, because Abigail stopped her crying instantly and pulled back from Sophie, looking directly in her face. Something about the way that Abigail looked at her made Sophie's stomach tighten on itself. 'What Abigail? Why are you looking at me like that?' Sophie leant forward on her hands to get closer to her face.

'You don't know, do you?' Abigail looked more worried than Sophie had seen her the night of the fire ritual.

'Abigail, you're scaring me. What do you mean?'

'Alex, your husband?'

'How do you know his name?'

'He's one of us. He's one of our group— The Tens.'

'Bullshit. Absolute bullshit.'

'It's true, I swear on Venus.' Abigail held her hands in a prayer.

'You're just making that up so I give up hope of being found and embrace this place,' Sophie swiped her arm around the room.

'Oh no. You truly didn't know.'

Sophie slapped Abigail across the face. Abigail rubbed both hands on the cheek she'd slapped.

'Don't you fucking spread shit about my husband

Abigail. You really are one of them!' She pointed towards the door.

'Sophie, I swear it's true! He's been part of us since before I can remember! I swear, I swear.' Abigail's eyes bulged, rimmed with aubergine.

The women stared at each other in silence, a heat building between them and scorching both their faces.

'Get the fuck away from me,' Sophie spat at her. She pushed her feet into the ground and crab-walked backwards to the other side of the shed, where she didn't have to look at Abigail. Abigail stopped begging and became silent, standing up and trying the door again. Which was still locked. Sophie watched her with hatred seething through her and she wondered why she had pitied her at all. This girl was not the delicate sylph that she had pretended to be, but rather, just as manipulative as the rest of the group. A group who lived in tents in the middle of a field and shared some kind of mass delusion that they could not be talked out of.

Sophie let images flick through her mind—people on the news that lived this way, sharing the same dangerous and unfounded beliefs, performed harmful rituals... none of it ended well. People always ended up abused or dead. Sophie's chest started to smart as it occurred to her that she was likely to die here, in this camp surrounded by these asinine people who didn't care about her. And she thought of the people that did care about her. It was excruciating to face such a tiny list of people. A list of no one. Carla never cared for her. What's worse is that up until a few days ago, Sophie faithfully assumed she cared about her the most. But, what she could deduce from the conversation she overheard, was that it was all some kind of hatched plan to extract information out of her. Bree cared about her, albeit briefly. But Sophie had put her off with her odd behaviour and she would have happily left her life as if she had never entered at all. Alex, well he clearly didn't care about her if he could just vanish and never contact her. And so, Sophie cried. Heart-wrenching sobs that hurt her throat. She cried for the fact that she would die as alone as she had lived.

Sophie lifted her head when she heard the sound of tumbling metal: Abigail was fumbling through some of the small wooden carved boxes. Abigail pulled something small and round out of one of the boxes. It was a key! Sophie wiped her face and stood up to ready herself. She was determined not to let Abigail get out without tagging along also, even if she had to hurt Abigail to do so.

But Abigail didn't walk to the door, instead, she strode over to Sophie and placed the key in her hand. Speechless, she looked at the key. As she looked at it and felt the cool sharpness of it, she realised it wasn't a key at all. Instead, it was a solitary keyring. A keyring that she kept seeing. The same sort of keyring that both Carla and Alex had. 'Sophie...' Abigail couldn't finish her sentence. She didn't know how. She didn't have to though because Sophie knew when she felt the stony metal oblong press into the palm of her hand and when she ran her thumb over the etching of the cross. Which was never a cross at all. But an "X". Abigail gingerly lifted Sophie's elbow and placed her forefinger on her new burn scar, slowly touching it in a circle. It was the same "X".

The keyring dropped to the cement floor with a hollow ting. 'How could I not have known he was in a fucking cult the entire time we were married? Like, how dumb can I be?'

'Sophie, you mustn't blame yourself. There is so much we are blind to when we know it will hurt us. Besides, we spent a lot of time with Alex casting blindness spells so you would deliberately not see that he was part of us, The Tens.' The look of pity on Abigail's face was almost excruciating.

'But how could he have been living out here, when I know for a fact he was living with me. We barely spent any time apart, for goodness sake!'

'That's true. He didn't live with us since you two moved in together. We would see him occasionally. When he reported back.'

Sophie's head swam. 'What do you mean, reported back?'

'Oh nothing, that's not what I meant. Sorry, I...' Abigail shrugged.

'Am I some kind of project for you all? Why me? Are you trying to recruit me?'

'No, not really. It's hard to explain. It's just...' again Abigail couldn't locate the words.

Sophie wanted to know more, wanted Abigail to be straight with her but the crushing realisation that Alex was part of a cult hit her hard.

'Abigail, please tell me. You must tell me this, please...' Sophie grabbed the front of her top desperately. 'Did he... ever love me?'

'I don't know. I assume so. I didn't have much to do with him. I did overhear Clive and Carla talking about how they were losing him. So maybe he was thinking about quitting. For you.' The small flake of hope that came with those words was a respite to Sophie, even if Abigail was lying. If it was even possible that Abigail could lie. She wore innocence like armour.

'I mean, I find it just so hard to believe that my Alex was into spells and believing that Venus was a planet to be revered. He used to squirm any time I mentioned anything vaguely supernatural.' And as the realisation hit, Sophie mouthed the word 'oh,' and put her head in her heads for what seemed like hours. 'Where is he then? Can I see him? Please Abigail, if I could just talk to him...'

'I honestly don't know. But it's not looking good. He hasn't been here for a few months now. I've feared the worst. As I said, I didn't know him that well but he was always kind to me. He has the same kindness in his eyes that you do. I don't want anything bad to have happened to him. But it's not above... them... this place.'

'What do you mean?'

'I shouldn't say. It's speculation, really. I don't

know it for real. But...' Abigail tossed up whether to tell Sophie or not but a cock of Sophie's head meant she'd already gone too far.

'There have been insinuations that people can be abolished if they don't place nicely. It's supposed to have happened before.'

'Oh, I believe it, Abigail. The way that I overhead Carla and Clive talking, I definitely believe it. And I'm next on their hit list, I would suspect. Do you think they... with Alex?'

'I don't know. He might have genuinely gone into hiding. It's all possible.'

'Would they hurt you, Abigail?'

'I don't know. They haven't so far. Unless you count the times they've admonished me for not following along and doing what I'm supposed to. There was a time when I was ordered to kill some birds by snapping their necks with my hands and I just couldn't! How could they ask me to do such a thing? Take a fragile life with my bare hands like it was as simple as picking up a stone. I thought they didn't want to hurt you either but it doesn't seem to be working.'

'What doesn't seem to be working? Why am I here Abigail?'

Abigail looked pained. She looked to the door and then towards the ceiling, which felt darker and lower than when they first came in. 'You have to take me with you,' she suddenly declared. 'We have to bust out of here. I want to come to the city with you. You can't leave me here.'

Ignoring her please, Sophie's voice dropped low. 'Abigail, why me?'

'Tell me you'll take me first.'

'Okay, okay, tell me and then we'll try and get out of here. Somehow.' Sophie wasn't lying, she couldn't leave this precious soul here to face the nature of this cruelness. Even if the city was going to be far too cruel for her anyway. A choice between two cruelties; what else could she do?

'You are chosen.'

Sophie couldn't help herself and she let out a laugh. 'Oh yeah, a regular Jesus I am.'

'You have the inherent alchemy that they need and they want to mine from you. To complete their plan.'

'I'm sorry but that's just absolutely absurd. I'm no more magical than a glass of water.'

'Sophie, you can't see it because you've been drugged and cast spells upon and gaslighted to believe that you are less than ordinary. But we've been taught from birth that you are the missing link. The alchemy cross mark.'

A fresh wave of pity rose up through her. This unkind group had brainwashed poor Abigail to not only believe in magic and spells and stuff of child-hood fantasies but that Sophie was something special.

Abigail seemed to be waiting for Sophie to take it all in.

'We really do have to get out of here. They are probably going to kill us, Abigail.'

She nodded silently whilst Sophie pushed herself up and doddered over to the shelves. Picking up a small box, she upended the twigs of rosemary to the floor and stepped over them with her good leg which was returning to almost full function, whilst her other leg took its time catching up. Lifting up the box in both hands she brought it down hard on the shed door latch, smashing it furiously in the hope it would release and let them out. But all it achieved was noise.

'Stop! Stop it. You'll make them come and tell us off,' Abigail was visibly afraid. Sophie discarded the box with a toss to the side. It skittered across the cement floor and stopped against one wall.

'But how are we going to get out of here, Abigail? We probably don't have much time.'

Abigail had sought out one of the rusty brown books from the shelf which made Sophie laugh with antipathy. 'You're not seriously suggesting that the book will help us in a time like this? The book— and the irrational idiots that believe in its tales— are the reason we are in here. Quick, flip to the page about being held hostage in a shed!' Sophie's derision was bordering on mean.

But Abigail ignored her and kept thumbing through the pages determinedly. 'There WILL be something in here to help us, there WILL. I just know it.'

Sophie shrugged at her and continued to explore the contents of the shed to aid in their escape. She shook her head in frustration at the useless herbs and picked up a small ornate metal pouch-shaped object, mainly for its beauty. It was made of brass or copper and eye-catching patterns and an image had been pressed into the object. Sophie ran her finger over the resting dog, which was shrouded by a garland and small birds, like those helpful animated ones that dressed Cinderella and were every kid's fantasy emblem of being a princess. There were several of the same objects and then nothing but more fresh and dried herbs on the shelf before her.

'Any luck?' turning back to Abigail, she said.

'Well, nothing specific but it's not always about specificity. Grab one of the books and help me look through. There has to be some kind of magic that can help us out here.'

'Hmm. I don't really think the book is going to save us, Abigail. But let me think about things a bit,' she plonked herself down and watched over Abigail's shoulder as she methodically turned and scanned the pages with her finger. The writing did have a magnetic quality which lulled Sophie into a small daze to the point where she almost forgot that she was in danger.

'I am absolutely exhausted, I just realised. I have nothing left in me. Maybe it's just better if we beg to be let out?' Sophie questioned.

'And then what?'

'Well, then if successful, I'll go back into my tent and I'll try to escape from there.'

'And then what will happen to me?'

'I'll come back for you.'

Abigail looked horrified. 'No! You mustn't leave without me. You won't come back for me and it won't be long before they do something wicked to me anyway. I don't follow protocol and I'm an outcast here. They are dying for an excuse to get rid of the deadwood that is me. Please don't leave me here. We have to get out of this shed and sneak away. Together.'

Sophie knew she was right and couldn't leave her to face the consequences on her own. 'Okay, you're right. I'll look after you. I promise. But how are we going to get out of here? What about one of the others? Surely there is someone willing to help you?'

'Honestly, the only people out of the whole group that have ever shown me kindness are you and Alex. The others will turn on me for their own gain without a second's hesitation. They will not even notice that I am missing.'

The room felt silent with impossibility. A space where all hope had whooshed out of the air and far away. Sophie slumped her shoulders with the weight.

'I have an idea,' Abigail said desperately. 'Magic works with emotion, right. And you are supposedly the alchemy cross mark. What if... hear me out... we just channelled a whole bunch of emotion and blasted the shed wall off?'

'That's absurd,' Sophie laughed.

'More absurd than being locked in a shed in the

middle of nowhere and having your arm thrust into a fire and then healed the next day?' Abigail flung her words at Sophie.

'No, I suppose you're right. What should I do then?'

'Okay, muster up some memories and strong feelings. Be angry that you are locked here, away from home. Really dive into the betrayal that Alex had deceived you all these years about who he really was and then left you on your own. Summon the deception of Carla, getting her to reveal your innermost turmoil, telling you about the nightmares, all under the guise of help but really it was to manipulate you and report back to us.'

Sophie nodded; all these scenarios were effortless to conjure.

'And finally, really feel the intensity of the loneliness that you feel. That you have always felt. That you believe you will always feel.'

Abigail's astuteness punched her in the guts and she wailed with an emotional pain she had been holding onto since her parents had died.

Abigail's soft voice floated around her head. 'That's it, use those feelings as a source of power. Now direct your feelings towards blowing open the door. You can do this!'

After each upsurge of sobs, Sophie felt more exhausted than she had ever felt in her life. Even after being drugged. Until eventually, she slowed down to a few small sniffles, her arms so heavy they could only lay on the ground.

'I'm sorry,' she whispered to Abigail.

'It was worth a try,' Abigail said quietly.

Violet half-moons had formed under Abigail's eyes and she tapped her fingernails together. The two leant into one another, slumped over, arms around each other.

'How about we just rest and get some sleep? Who knows what could happen later? Maybe Carla will free us tomorrow?' Sophie croaked with false optimism, wanting to buoy Abigail's spirits up and protect the young starling. Sophie patted her lap and Abigail snuggled her head into it. The warmth seeped through to Sophie's thighs and it stirred more than protection, more than fear. It woke a love and care that she had only ever reserved for Alex. And she was convinced that she felt it back. Abigail was someone to care about, that cared for her in return.

She wasn't sure if Abigail was asleep but they both acted as if, their only chance at calm. Perhaps before the storm. Or perhaps a restorative tonic. She reached for the book that had been discarded by her legs. The writing, the symbols, the textured cover had started to become familiar, although the incredulity that people would take it for more than someone's ridiculous diary and made her shudder. There were no answers in the book but there were clues on how Carla and Clive thought. Their whole philosophy was contained in the pages and if Sophie studied them enough to understand how their psychology played out, maybe she could work out how to appeal to their worshipping sensibilities. And persuade them to let her go back to her life.

Sophie winced when she landed on the fire ritual page: 'A holy divinity and preparation enchantment to ensure those who pledge themselves and follow the ways of The Tens will be ready for the day when Venus and Earth meld. Only those who can either withstand or heal rapidly from Venus' insufferable heat will survive and be able to exist in The New Way, The Venus Way. Anyone who does not heal overnight from this trial will certainly fare no well when the great almighty Venus latches back to Earth. The sulphur will burn through the lungs and the flesh will be heat stripped from the bones. You must waste no time performing this ritual, for Venus is coming sooner than you think. There is no age too young to conduct this powerful ceremony.'

Sophie thought of the baby that Carla wanted Abigail to burn and she wondered where it was. There was no way it was safe from harm, even if they never put it through this inhumane ritual. Growing up in a cult, The Tens as they seemed to call themselves, would leave one unfit; a brittle caged bird. Like Abigail. Sophie pictured Abigail in the outside world and knew that she would not be able to protect her, even there. In her mind, she saw her crying from the overwhelm and being left alone for more than a few hours or crumbling apart at the horror that the daily news spouted. This world was not created for someone like Abigail and she hated Clive and Carla even more for bringing Abigail up this way and belonging nowhere.

Hastily, she flipped the page away from the unease of the fire ritual. And what greeted her next made her stare in wonderment. A double-page spread of beautiful flying blackbirds dotted around the border, standing strong against the creaminess of the pages. Some mid-flight, some standing on their forked legs and some carrying debris in their beaks, on their way back to their nest. Over the birds, she traced her finger around the paper, just knowing they had something to tell her. Skimming her eyes over the page, the quaint symbol stood out directly in the middle. It was a more complex symbol than any she had seen in the book or dotted around the camp's items. Noticing now that symbols were what she was seeing all along: on the ceramic canisters in the shed, marked on several trees, on the sides of saucepans held over the fire... made to look like innocuous squiggles, Sophie thought they were anything but seeing as they formed part of a caustic ideology. She looked at one of the ceramic urns again. It had an "X" engraved in it. The roman numeral for ten. It was hard to unsee now. Alex's keyring, the jumpers, Carla's number plate... all of it was staring her in the face. A week ago, Sophie would have convinced herself that she was descending into lunacy if she kept seeing symbols. But all it took was one person, Abigail in all her innocence, to show her that she wasn't going insane.

The symbol in the book comprised of strokes and bubbles and half circles and had indentations like rivets that suggested the lines had been drawn over and over.

Sophie leant over Abigail's face to see if she was awake and noticed her eyes were already open. There was a soft greyness to them, like a lake had been draining away and there was nothing left to see but the lake bed. 'Sweetheart, what does this symbol mean?'

Abigail half-heartedly shifted her body to sit up-right and traced her finger along the symbol. She was about to say that she had no idea when it made sense. 'Follow the birds,' she said nonchalantly.

'What does that mean? Does that make any sense to you?'

'It just means... I don't know... follow the birds.' Abigail shrugged and laid her head back down in defeat.

So, Sophie searched the birds' flight path, looking for clues, looking for anything out of the ordin-ary that might give her insight into what Clive and Carla were planning to do next. What they had in store for her. But the birds went around and around in a circle on the page and just ended up frustrating Sophie more than ever. Her mind drifted back to the dead birds that kept accumu-lating at her house. The ones that met their match with the clear windows. The sparrow that flew into her tent. The tiny birds that adorned the cop-per cases she spied on the shelf earlier. The cases!

She leapt up and Abigail bounced off her. 'Abigail, what are these?' Grabbing the horned shaped ornaments in both hands she shoved them in her friend's face.

'Careful!' Abigail shrieked. 'They are canisters of gunpowder. The ancients believed they were a key ingredient to immortality. We use it in spells.' And as Abigail let out the last syllable, they both shared an idea at the same time, eyes and mouths agape.

'Let's blow the door off!'

'Do you really think we can?'

'We need some matches or something to light them. And if there's any fertiliser in here, that would be even better!'

Abigail nodded and starting searching as Sophie inspected the door. Where could she place them to have the most effect, without injuring themselves?

'Sophie, what does fertiliser look like?'

'I really don't know actually. Maybe we can try any kind of liquid you find?'

'We have this diesel here for the vehicle we used to have. Will that work?'

'We're going to have to try. Be careful with it! Move it gently near the door but not the exact spot until we are ready to go. When do you think the best time to do this is?'

Abigail contemplated. 'Now?'

'What about if we wait a bit. Lull them into a false sense of security. Maybe dinner time before it gets dark? Surely they'll be busier?'

'Okay but we must do it today. I don't want to wake

up tomorrow and be subject to their wickedness tomorrow. I know what they're capable of.'

'I'm sure you do.'

'If they come back and feed us, they will give us the paralysing potion again. Or the memory loss thing.'

'Memory loss thing?'

'Yeah, you know...' Abigail realised her mistake and busied herself careful shifting the plastic jerry can of fuel.

'Abigail. I do not know. Tell me about this memory loss thing.' Sophie folded her arms.

Abigail chewed her lip and squished her face up, like a jellyfish about to jettison forward.

'Have you noticed strange things since your thirtieth birthday?'

'Well, my husband left me not long after, so yeah. You could say that.'

'Right. But even before then, did your nightmares increase? Did you hear voices? Did you always feel a little bit like you were going crazy?'

'Not just a little bit. I went full-blown crazy. I thought I could fly! I tried to jump off a fucking balcony Abigail. Hence why I started the sessions with Carla. What are you telling me, Abigail?'

'It was all orchestrated. When you were little, very little, you were fed the memory loss supplement. It's like a strong version of the copper water we use. You were probably no more than four or five. So lore has it.'

'I'm sorry, what? How do you know all this? Did

Alex tell you this?'

'Sophie...' Abigail's face crumpled with earnest and she fiddled with her hair. 'You were born here. You were fed this potent potion to repress your memories of this place as an experiment and keep you somewhat obscured from this world. Then released into the wild, as it were. The Seniors wanted to see how effective the memory potion really was. It was always designed to wear off on your thirtieth birthday. And it sounds like your inherent magical abilities that were dormant, aided by complete amnesia, started to sprout to life. To someone who is not of the alchemical persuasion this looks, unequivocally, like madness. We were so excited when Alex reported that you had started to regain some of your mystical abilities, although you had no idea they were such. Everything we had been waiting for: the crosshatch, the missing link, to preparing ourselves for Venus' return was happening. But what we weren't counting on was you discovering us before we brought you here. Talk about divinity! It really rushed us and we made mistakes in our hastiness. We missed our first window when Venus was in Retrograde.'

Sophie couldn't help herself but look at Abigail like she was the unhinged one. The sweet girl had no reason to fib to her but she had obviously been fed a cacophony of lies, which again tugged on her heartstrings. There was more damage than she first thought.

'I know you don't believe me. I don't know how to

convince you that it's true. And you don't have to believe it. But doesn't it feel like peace to have some semblance of an explanation why you suddenly started experiencing weirdness out of nowhere?'

Abigail was right. Half the painful battle of her deteriorating mental health was the inability to lay blame, to place a reason where it all started to unfurl. It was part of the appeal why she kept going back to therapy with Carla. And why she had to desperately find Alex instead of letting him go. Sophie was convinced that if she could just find a reason why she was unravelling, that she would be able to mitigate it: take the right vitamins, learn the right cognitive techniques, eliminate the stressors... and she would be fine. But the needle kept swaying too wildly for it to land on the answer.

'So, I'm not mad? Everything that has been telling me that I've been losing my mind has actually been happening to me? Even feeling sick all the time? That's because you lot have been slowly destroying me through Alex?' Sophie felt dizzy and a realisation took hold of her. As the screen to reality became less grubby, she saw that a whole group of people had been conspiring against her and there was no way she could have seen that. The whole time she thought was descending into some kind of irrecoverable madness.

A chill swept through Sophie like someone had opened a window. 'When you say I was born here, do you mean that I was born in this place?'

'As far as I know. It was a few years before I was

born, but like me, you were born here.'

'That's impossible. My parents...'

Abigail gave her a sympathetic look.

'Are you saying my parents were part of this heinous tribe?'

'Yes, Sophie I believe so. They were valued and loved. Particularly for creating our first member born into The Tens.'

'Why the hell would they choose to be part of this nonsense?' Sophie was outraged.

'I can't really be sure of their reasons. But I do know that a lot of people find genuine appeal in being part of a culture that takes care of their own. You heard Jesse's story. Everyone is very loved here, even if you can't see it yet. As long as we follow the book and what Carla says, then life can be filled with safety, security and wonderment. And the pull of reconnecting again to Venus is powerful.'

'Did you know that my parents died in a car crash?'

Abigail stared at Sophie, waiting patiently. And then the penny dropped. All these realisations tumbled one after the other. And yet, a strange sense of understanding came with them. It was as if this was the information she had been waiting for her whole life.

'It wasn't an accident, was it Abigail?'

'I don't think so, from what I've been told. Carla and Clive threaten us with the tale all the time. It's a way to make sure we are too scared to leave. Your parents were doing the right thing, they wanted to take you away and live in the world again. They didn't want you to be subject to whatever Carla had planned for you. They had no hope, really. The day of their crash, they were all set to speed away with you in the backseat. But the car flipped out of control, which Clive still purports was the doing of the Wild Woman. Your parents were killed instantly but you, well you were reportedly untouched and unphased, sitting quietly like a ghost in the back. This was further testament to how we revered you as a magical one. Carla and Clive must have slipped you the memory concoction before the emergency crew arrived and then skulked back into the clearing. It's nothing short of miraculous that, through a series of events, you found your way back to us.'

'I was raised in this place? Until I was five?'

'Yes. And because you were young, you were more receptive to the alchemical teachings. But more than that, we knew you had something special within you. At least, some of us did. Those of us who worked more closely with you have regaled us time and time again. Most of the commune didn't even realise that most of the abilities you already held within you at the time. That you could magnify any experience more than anyone. You are the crosshatch.'

There was nowhere for Sophie to put this information. She felt like it wasn't even hers to store away. If any of it was true, it wouldn't just explain the way everyone at the camp looked at her but explained so very much in her life. Her lifelong sensitivity to being Ghost Girl, the hallucinations, hair loss, the missing parts of her childhood and nightmares. 'So why do Carla and Clive want to kill me? If I'm their supposed key?'

'Crosshatch,' she corrected. 'I don't really know. I think Carla discovered in your sessions that you weren't as powerful as they had anticipated. It would have been a huge letdown for everyone, nearly thirty years in the making. Carla hates to be wrong. I've never seen her admit to being wrong. That's why she keeps Clive around her, he always tells her she is right and agrees with everything she says. Or mostly does. They don't really have a choice but to silence you for good.'

Sophie contemplated her, her nose pressing back into itself. Unconsciously, she pressed at her fire scar hoping a dull ache would show itself but nothing came. It was no more than a scar, as if she had acquired it in teenagerhood. There was no guarantee that she had not descended further into the abyss of insanity and everything she was experiencing was a carefully constructed delusion. She could be tucked up at home in bed, for all she really knew. 'How do I know any of it is real?'

'Well, you don't. But there are some things that you could consider. Has the consistency of this experience been the same the whole time you've been here? Do you understand the difference between right and wrong and want to get away to preserve your own life?'

Sophie nodded but remained sceptical.

'It's real Sophie. It's quaint and it's queer and it's something society shuns as madness. But it's real. All that I've told you, it has happened to you. Whether you believe in the Venus stuff— I know that even I, who has been taught nothing else have questioned it very occasionally— is entirely up to you. Either way, you have to escape.'

Abigail's voice lowered and deepened. She was no longer the Abigail that Sophie knew. It was as if someone was speaking through her. Abigail's wisdom shot through her and as she talked, she saw the face of another superimpose over hers. A face that seemed familiar but one that she had never seen in the flesh. Sophie thought she recognised it from the book.

'Carla really is sinister, isn't she?' Sophie posited.

'Since you have come here, I have seen that more and more. I spent most of my childhood not even questioning so. But then I started to have dreams about Madame Maudelynne— the creator of The Tens— and she would tell me that "not everything is as it seems" and that I "didn't have to believe what I was told". I, too, thought I was going insane at first and that I just had to believe harder, worship harder, be more involved in ritual. But when you came, hearing you talk about another way, another life, another world... I knew that Madame Maudelynne was sending me a message through time, through space, through dimensions, to listen to my heart and question what the Seniors, and even the book, told us.'

Sophie thought of the pages in the book that she recognised. *Madame Maudelynne and The New Way,* they were titled. Madame Maudelynne was a sought after psychic reader who joined a beloved travelling circus in the 1860s. After a bout of insanity, she started believing that Venus was coming to join with earth and that people needed to prepare for the new way through the worshipping of copper and its supposed alchemical properties. And thus, she formed The Tens.

Sophie sniffed at the irony that all three women questioned their sanity and their own worlds. They were all bound by the thread of mysticism, disguised as insanity.

There was a parallel and familiarity that Sophie witness in Abigail and she wasn't too proud to admit that she liked it. 'Thank you for telling me all this Abigail. I'm not sure I can truly believe any of it yet but I owe it to you to help you discover a new world. One where you are free to question things without the crushing weight of believing you're insane. There's a whole, beautiful world out there just waiting for you. You're going to love it! You can go to classes and learn just about anything you want to. Or go to a supermarket and choose just about any kind of item you can think of. From pre-chopped onions to complete roast chicken meals, already cooked. Have you ever watched TV?' 'No but I have heard of it. And I saw it briefly in a window when I visited the city with Clive once.'

'Oh, you are going to love it! There are so many

stories and shows on TV, you can watch what you want, whenever you feel like it. Best of all, no one is going to make you put fire on yourself.'

Abigail smiled at her with a warmth that radiated outwards. 'It sounds overwhelming! Maybe a little at a time?'

'Of course. You have the rest of your life to discover things.'

CHAPTER
THIRTY TWO

I n all her serenity, Abigail ushered Sophie over. 'Come on, let's do this now. It's time to break free.' Sophie knew she was talking about the shed but suspected she was talking about more.

Abigail splashed a little of the fuel at the base of the shed wall, far enough away from the door so they could escape without inhaling too much smoke or getting caught in the explosion. The acrid tang wafted up at her and gave her a kick of energy.

'Be ready to make an absolute run for it when this goes off,' Abigail warned.

Sophie shook her legs out, trying to rid them of the last bouts of pins and needles and numbness.

'Give them to me,' Abigail gestured at the gunpowder cases and Sophie obeyed. The frail bird that Abigail was had left her and she had transformed into a plight of power and direction. Sophie found herself admiring her.

'Okay, so when this goes off, it's going to leave a hole which is hopefully going to be big enough for both of us to squeeze through. Then we just run. Flat out.'

Sophie grabbed one of the ugly Tens jumpers and ripped of each sleeve, fastening one around Abigail's nose and mouth and one around her own. The rest of the jumper she soaked in fuel and laid in a line from the faded jerry can towards where they both stood a few metres away. A single nod let Abigail know she was ready.

'Now what?'

They both looked around them desperate to find something to light the fuel. Suddenly, Sophie gasps and reaches into her pants. The matches that she found near the bird were thankfully hidden deep down in her pocket. She pulls the thin packet out triumphantly.

Abigail held out her hand and Sophie lobbed them straight into the centre of her palm. The first match struck out and went nowhere. The second took but didn't light the jumper. There were two remaining matches and both didn't like their chances. Abigail crossed her fingers and held them up to Sophie and lit one of the remaining matches. The movement slowed down, slower than time itself. In a perfect arc, Abigail shot the lit match through the air and into the mouth of the jerry can. Sophie watched it, mouth agape. At first, nothing happened. There was a horrid, empty second where despair fell out of both their bodies. But all at once, the can exploded into a perfect cylinder of fire. And then it met the gunpowder and it cracked as it ricocheted off the shed wall.

Through the sluggish smoke, they watched a hole appear before them filling with inviting twilight. It was small, so they would have to crouch but they could get out.

'Go!' Abigail demanded.

Sophie rushed forth, eyes squeezed shut against the smoke and launched herself, hands first, at the opening. Searing agony shot through her hands as they hit the hot iron and then the scalding ground and she screamed into the makeshift mask. When she could manage to open an eye, she saw trees in the distance. That was the first thing she noticed. Greenery, beckoning her away from a place that did nothing but, if Abigail was right, poison her from an early age. She scraped her belly along the hot concrete and felt the sharp lip of curled iron scrape across her back, through her clothes. Wiggling her hips through the opening, she crawled out onto the dirt outside, her legs unsteady and her lungs closing in on themselves. Rolling to the side, to make room for Abigail, she used her elbows to push herself up and looked around, terrified that Clive or Carla would see her. But there was no one around and so she bolted towards the closest set of trees.

Sophie pressed her back against a Mallee gum and ripped her mask down with her injured hands as parts of her body battled for attention in their agony. Struggling for breath and with eyes full of clouds, she arched her head around to see if Abigail had followed her.

Sophie screamed into her hands when she saw what was unfolding at the shed. Abigail was half-way through the hole and Carla had grabbed her by the neck shaking her roughly. Even through the whining of her ears, she could hear Carla's ad-monishment. She had yanked Abigail all the way through the shed's hole and to the ground, where she hunched over something small cradled in her arms. Abigail looked so tiny, like she could have disappeared into the ground. As Carla yelled at her, fury pouring from her mouth so much that her head looked like it was going to jerk clean off her body, Abigail stood purposefully. Proud of her de-fiance, Sophie willed her to run towards her, so they could escape together and she could fulfil her promise. But Abigail didn't run. Or even walk. She turned to the direction where Sophie was hiding and Sophie watched her mouth 'run' as she poured the contents of the red container over her head. Amid her confusion, Sophie stood still. Had Abi-gail changed her mind? Was she going to stay? Carla held up her hands and quickly walked back-wards and it was then that Sophie realised what the tiny scarlet thing pulsating in Abigail's hand was. The last match.

Sophie whipped her head around, back to the com-fort of the green trees, before she had to witness

Abigail being completely ravaged by flames. Gasping as she ran faster and harder than she ever, her lungs burned and her head swam. The shock of Abigail's sacrifice spurred her to run further and faster than she knew herself to be capable of.

CHAPTER
THIRTY THREE

Pumping her numb legs into the ground, Sophie kept expecting to reach the fence, the same one that lined her safety. That was the threshold from crossing over from a woman whose husband had left her to one that had stumbled upon a cult that had enslaved her, her whole life. But the fence didn't show up and she had no idea where she was going. The shock pumped through her and the woodland turned into obsidian silhouettes against the dusk sky. It wasn't just the looming night that was scaring her. What had been a breeze had started to develop into a promise of a sinister wind. The trees rustled so much that they sounded like monsters or waves of infrequent TV static. The wind quickly became an animal. Sophie could have stood at the top of the rise and not hear anyone shout her name over it. It howled and emptied its lungs and roared to a crescendo and then died off like it never existed.

Sophie felt a whoosh of air all around her, simultaneously pushing her down and lifting her up. It felt so windy that her hearing was washed out and her hair flapped in her face, like she was plummeting down an endless slippery slide.

Suddenly, the space around her seemed to expand, she felt like she was being sucked backwards. Everything around her turned midnight blue punctuated with streaks of electric white. Terror tugged at the nape of her neck through the chill of the air. Somehow, Sophie knew what she was approaching.

A beast stood on a small rise in the ground. The beast's hair looked like a wobbly flame with tight spiralled curls dwarfing its head, which arched all over to one side, like a wave about to break. The figure was clad in a second skin of the blackest material, that shone purple when it— when she— arched her back. The material clung to her body and dripped and draped from her limbs, back and shoulders. The only bit of skin exposed her hands, neck and face, bore a sheen so delicate, so frighteningly reflective that it set her hair alight even more.

The Wild Woman curved until Sophie thought she might break in two and clutched at her throat, swathes of material flapping at her fingers, her nails pointy and long and the colour of menses blood. Arching the way she was made her look like a tree. A bent plane tree, blackened out at sunset, abandoned by its leaves, the only colour a brush of remaining flame-red leaves curled over at the top.

This creature was partly petrifying and mostly mesmerising. Compelled, Sophie strode towards her, ready to undo the hallucination. To confront her and all that she stood for.

'Come to me, come to me, come to me,' her beckons swirled in the air, wrapping around Sophie's waist and pulling her towards her. The closer she got, the more she could see her face with every flicker of light and movement, alternating between the smooth skin of youth and the crinkly and drawn face of a crone. The Wild Woman's limbs were so spindly they looked as if they were twigs and she watched her fingers with their spider-like movements with fascination. Trying to catch the woman's invisible gaze, Sophie splayed her open hands towards the woman. 'Do you... need something?' Unsure whether she should be asking or offering.

'Stand still.' The woman screeched in time with a piercing thunder crack. Sophie obeyed, enjoying the uncanny feeling of a thunderstorm that she unwittingly yearned for. One that would break all the pressure that her body and soul contained. The sky cracked again and shards of lightning broke up the indigo dusk; white-hot snakes of light streamed downwards behind her, illuminating her silhouette so all Sophie could see was darkness and a bush of scarlet hair.

With the next flash, she had disappeared and the storm dropped instantly. And in swooped a sticky euphoria. Behind where the woman had been standing was a pale white reflection, glowing through the grim night. Sophie no longer cared if it was the Wild Woman entrapping her or a torch-light of one of The Tens. If they caught her there would be no mercy, she was certain. And she was so drained from everything she had been told and everything that she had seen that she had nothing left to fight with. There was no barometer for real-ity or insanity anymore, so she ambled towards the echo of light.

The closer she got to the wide light figure, the more she slowed down. For as she stood two metres away from it, she knew exactly what it was. An object she had been familiar with her whole life. Something that had terrorised her so acutely that to come upon it at a time like now, confused her. Her body hurtled forward as she rested her forehead on the big white rock from her night-mares, its coolness a balm that took away some of the burning pain and the horror of what Abigail had done to herself.

The rock could not save her, she knew that and it wouldn't be long before one of the campers would discover her but she could not ignore that she had foretold the sighting of the rock and it had tran-spired into her life.

And just like in her nightmares those many times when she jolted away in a damp film, came the laughter. It rolled around her, chasing itself with an echo. But the laughter was different than in her dreams, it was less tinny, less menacing. It wasn't exactly comical either. The laughter flew around her head and she held her breath, fearing that Carla had caught up to her. Amid the laughter, she heard a familiar sound: flapping. The tap of a wing on a feathered body made her sag to her knees with relief and she looked up, her eyes scouring the treetops. There were birds laughing at her. Their raucous caws were almost mirthful to her now. Pressing her forehead and ravaged palms to the rock, as she knelt before it, her shoulders shrugged in laughter at the fancy of these voyeuristic characters that had been with her every step of the way. Not quite helpful and not quite harmful but nevertheless, they had been tracking her all along.

Her stomach softened as she relaxed to catch her breath, listening to the gentler whistling wind and the boisterous birds. Just as Sophie was deciding her next move, whether to hide or keep walking through the cold night, a concrete hand clamped on her shoulder and she tensed back up. A bony thumb pressed into her flesh. They had finally caught up with her.

CHAPTER
THIRTY FOUR

'Sophie?' A mellifluous voice questioned. Turning her head to face the soft voice in amazement, Sophie saw her beloved friend Bree standing over her. 'Bree?'

Bree took three steps back and lifted a black box to her mouth and mouthed words into it. Bree had lost her suburban mum look and sported more urban attire, with black utility pants and boots and a khaki zipped-up bomber jacket. 'It's okay honey, you're okay,' she crouched down to Sophie's height and looked at her reassuringly as several men swam in from behind trees.

Sophie noticed the glint of her decorated badge clipped to the top of her waistband and looked back up to her eyes. 'What are you doing here?' Was all Sophie could get out in between raspy breaths.

'I'm a detective, Sophie. I've been part of an undercover operation to bust apart a camp that I found your name associated with. Unfortunately, that meant I've had to be under the guise of friendship whilst I collected more information about these bastards. Although I wish it wasn't. We're gonna get you to safety real quick but can you do me a favour and tell me which way you came from?'

Sophie wept and pointed back into the trees where she came from and watched four indistinguishable police officers trot off in that direction. Bree winced as she spotted Sophie's burnt hands.

'It's okay Sophie, you're safe now. I'm sorry that this escalated so much before I stepped in. You've been missing for a few days and it was never my intention to let it get so far before I pulled the plug on their bullshit.'

Sophie could do nothing but cry, her tears falling heavy to the dirt below her.

'Let's get you into the vehicle and check those injuries out. I'll ride with you.'

Bree looked back to Sophie who was slumped in the back seat of the police car on the way to the hospital, her palms face up and looking angry with tangerine-coloured blisters.

'I must say our timing is exquisite, hun. We've been scouring around the area for about twenty-four hours now and there was not a trace. If it wasn't for me hearing you laughing to yourself, I may be searching for you for another day or two. I'm so glad we found you.'

Although Sophie felt duped by the charade that

Bree had put up with her to find The Tens, she felt like she was in safe hands. Anything to be away from that camp. She thought of Abigail and whimpered softly as she realised that Abigail could have been freed anyway if the police came upon them.

Bree looked down at her phone and thumped the dashboard with excitement. 'Just got a message hun, they've got them! You helped us, you really did. We've been on this hunt for years.'

'You mean you've arrested them? All of them?'

'Yep, all of them will be taken to the station for questioning and I'm confident the leaders, at the least, will be charged.'

They weren't going to come after her. Sophie was safe from them. She could return home and finally get better now that no one was poisoning her or trying to make her crazy.

'Why did you give me Carla's card that time?' Sophie was perplexed. How far back did Bree's influence go?

'I'm sorry that I had to throw you into the hornet's nest like that. But we weren't getting anywhere and we already had eyes on her but couldn't quite pin her for anything. I honestly didn't think they would go to such extremes. I thought you'd just give me snippets of information about her whenever we caught up for coffee. But you've helped us more than you can ever know. You truly have.'

'There's a baby.'

'What's that, hun?'

'They have a baby with them at the camp. They

wanted one of the girls... they wanted Abigail to burn her in the fire. You'll find Abigail's body there. She... you'll find her body there,' Sophie gulped back her words as she watched the scenery blur past her window.

'Oh, hun. You're going to be okay now. Our officers will make sure everyone is as safe as they can be.'

'Bree?'

'Yes, hun?'

'I think they also killed my parents too.' Bree mouthed silently, 'I know' and her face crumpled at Sophie.

As they pulled up to the hospital car park, Sophie noticed several white vans, cordoned off by police tape and a handful of officers casually waiting nearby. They looked up when they saw the car approaching. 'Did you...,' Sophie sighed to herself, self-conscious that her mind had been wobbly for so long. But she didn't have a lot to lose. 'Did you ever come by my house? With the van, I mean?'

'Yes. We did. And look, I'm sorry if this unnerved you, if you ever saw us. We tried to be as inconspicuous as possible. But it was part of the operation. We had to keep tabs on you. Initially, we weren't quite clear on the extent of your involvement.'

'I see.' Sophie should have been furious but all she felt was unreserved relief. She didn't hallucinate any of it: the van at the front of her house, the woman following her in the car, Bree giving her the cold shoulder when Sophie had busted her following her out the front of Carla's office. There was nothing wrong with her.

'Let's get you inside. There's a doctor waiting to see how much of the skin on your hands we can save. And a psychiatrist should you need one.'

For the first time in ages, Sophie felt like she was in her right mind. Even after all that she had been through.

CHAPTER
THIRTY FIVE

S ophie only allowed herself to watch a small bit of news coverage: the same footage they kept repeating which became synonymous with the arrests. A trail of people looking sheepishly at the ground, as they are walked towards vans, their hands cuffed. They all looked ridiculous in their matching jumpers, most of them barefoot and powerless, without the protection of their isolation and idiotic practices.

'A cult has been discovered in the woods of the farming region, known as The Tens, who have long believed that the planet Venus is going to somehow fuse with Earth and become one planet. Police have uncovered an illegal camp and have reported that cult members were consciously trying to poison themselves with the mineral copper, in order to prepare themselves for what they have dubbed,

The New Way,' the incredulity of every newsreader that reported the story said it all to Sophie. She was never the crazy one.

'Yoohoo,' Bree rapped at the front door.

'Coming,' Sophie announced from the kitchen where she stood in the warm glow of the sunshine and was smiling to herself. Since she'd returned home, the house felt less empty, even though it was just her there. She'd opened up the blinds and windows more, less fearful of what was plaguing her or that a bird was going to fly inside.

Sophie slid away the copy of *Venus* that she stole, hidden under her waistband the whole time and went to usher Bree inside for a warm coffee and equally warm chat.

'Their so-called alchemy is useless to them now,' Bree laughed at the TV screen playing in the background. 'Carla and Clive have been detained and are awaiting trial for trespassing and squatting and holding someone against their will, intentional administration of harmful substances, impersonating a psychologist and a few other little delights that we've chucked in there for good measure. Another team are investigating the link to your parents' death.' She winked at Sophie. But her smile changed when she noticed Sophie's hands. 'Your hands have healed so well!' Bree was visibly shocked. 'Lucky we took you straight to hospital, rather than the station.'

Sophie beamed but knew the real reason why her hands wore barely a glimpse of what they had been through. Sometimes, in certain lights, they shone a little silver, like a scar under moonlight or iridescent like mermaid's scales. It wasn't always that obvious though.

Bree sat down without invitation and Sophie followed suit. 'I'm afraid there's still no word on Alex. He just seemed to disappear into thin air. There's no trace of him back at the camp and no one there has revealed anything about where he might be. I even suspect they genuinely don't know. Tracing his phone has come up completely empty, it has been off for far too long. I'm so sorry but we just don't know where he is. I promise you that we will keep doing everything we know how to do to find him. It's just an unusual case. There are no traces of his whereabouts, no signs of which way he has gone and certainly no evidence that we've found a body to match his. You could take all these things as signs of hope. But rest assured, I will keep you informed every step of the way.'

Bree's seriousness didn't deter Sophie. It was clear she was good at her job. And whilst it absolutely confounded her that Alex could just disappear like that, she could have some understanding. She suspected he wanted to be safe, away from Carla and Clive. Perhaps he would show up now they were in jail. There were so many unanswered questions. But what Sophie knew was that she felt so much more solid in herself, even without Alex. For the first time in her life, she was relaxed and content, making friends with herself: madness, magic and all. Besides, she knew when she was ready for Alex to come back into her life, if she chose that's what she wanted, she knew she could make it happen.

Bree's tone and face softened. 'I've mainly come to see how you're doing Soph? I know I betrayed you and my involvement in this case was never fully disclosed initially but I honestly hope you can forgive me and we can truly be friends?' Bree's eyes were shining and she unconsciously placed a hand to her chest.

Sophie could read and feel the earnestness just pouring out of her. 'Yeah, I think I'd like that too, Bree. But we don't have to go back to those horrid groups, right?'

Bree chortled so hard that she had to put her mug down. 'Oh, geez they were terrible, weren't they? I'm embarrassed to say that we were barking up the wrong tree there. The unit had suspected the group was in some way connected to The Tens but it turns out they were just a bunch of whack-a-doo hippies! Another thing I have to apologise for, I guess.' She paused and sipped her coffee, taking in Sophie with her eyes. 'I really am keen to be your friend, Sophie. I really like you. And to prove it, I've asked my boss's wife to meet with you. She owns a little gallery smack bang in the middle of the city. Would you be interested in showing her your art?'

Sophie smiled directly at her. Since she'd been home, albeit without Alex, she'd been practising trusting herself and listening to what she really wanted, from deep inside of her. She could tell it was already taking effect because when she looked at Bree, everything inside of her said she was genuine: in her apology and in her gesture to help get her art sold. It felt right, all aligned, like there was nothing to fear. She followed that feeling. 'Oh Bree, I would love that. In fact, I've already been working on a new collection.' Sophie beckoned her into the dining room. 'It's called *Abigail's Liberty*.'

Spread across three easels and lining the floor and dining table were all sized canvasses that sported various birds of distinction. Each piece depicted the birds doing something meaningful, like they were trying to communicate through the pieces; with a slight cock of the head or gracefully midflight. Sophie was so proud of them. The pressure valve had been released enough for her to explode her art everywhere. As she had always wanted. The freedom was intoxicating; realising her imagined world onto paper was the best drug, or path to sanity, she believed existed. There was a silent and steady knowing within her that these pieces were the ones she'd been waiting her whole life to birth. The birds were uncaged.

The end.

LIKED THIS BOOK?

Please leave a positive review on Amazon and/or Goodreads as this helps other readers know this is a good read and it helps me sell more books!

Thank you

BOOKS BY THIS AUTHOR

The Business Psychic

Ruby is the most unlikely psychic ever— she figures she can just fake it until she makes it.

When Ruby unjustly gets fired from her job, her best friend suggests she try her hand at being a psychic. Despite having no abilities, Ruby agrees out of financial desperation. It's not long before the fancy tech company, Crichton Enterprises, mistakes her for a real psychic and hires her to help improve their business.

At her new job, she is so good at faking it that she starts to hear a voice which tells her what to do and starts having visions that have people thinking she's lost her damn mind. But then her favourite co-worker disappears and her paranormal skills are called upon to find out exactly where he is. As she goes looking for him, she uncovers more than she bargains for about Crichton Enterprises and puts herself in a world of danger.

Can Ruby save herself and help find her missing co-worker without people finding out that she's been faking it all along?

A paranormal cozy mystery with delightful characters and quippy lines that will keep you guessing.

Reviews
"The main character is sassy, and really relatable. Her accidental job as a psychic is pretty eventful, and I really enjoyed how that unfolded, and how the characters evolved. I'd definitely recommend this if you like a bit of intrigue, a lot of giggles, and an end that makes you go 'ohhhhhhh'."

"A great read with a tight, well written and entertaining storyline revolving around an engaging well developed protagonist. I devoured the book, enjoying it thoroughly from beginning to end."

Madame Maudelynne And The New Way

A FREE standalone gothic historical story just for you.

Madame Maudelynne was a sought after psychic

reader who joined a beloved travelling circus in the 1860s. It was in that very circus that she fell in love with her soul mate. Who wasn't human.

When her soul mate died, she slipped into a deep feverish fervour. And started channelling an important secret about what was coming... The New Way. From then on, she sees it as her mission to prepare people and the world for the coming of Venus and The New Way.

An intriguing short story for lovers of historical and occult or gothic fiction.

Venus is coming. Are you prepared?

Uneasy

Uneasy is a collection of dark short stories with an undercurrent of suburban ennui and the uneasiness that comes from ordinary life. The stories unearth all the darkness that we do not talk about but that still exists.

Featuring a signature darkness and poetic style, whilst tackling centuries old themes that are still relevant today, such as unrequited love, deep domestic unhappiness and the desperate and misguided strive for normality.

Including:

The War Gift
The Book of Elizabeth Purdon
The First Cloud
The Man in the Park
Left
Missing Marjorie
The Adjustment House
Ceramic Cliches.

Reviews

5/5
Beautifully written with such richness and intrigue, it left me wishing that this was not a book of "short" stories. Devoured this with solitary pleasure Waiting for her next book...
Janine

5/5
Gripping collection of short stories. Jones creates a rich, emotive and dark atmosphere sure to leave you a little uneasy.
Louise

Potent: Improve Your Website With Powerful Copywriting

You know deep down that a great website can be the key to higher sales and more leads and customers. So how are you supposed to create effective content if you don't have any idea what's involved? That's where this book steps in and holds your hand on the pathway to a better business.

Unpack copywriting secrets

Your website is your bread-and-butter so why take chances? Unpack the secrets to providing persuasive copy across your entire site that's powerful enough to knock someone off their chair. Plus, you'll get the lowdown on SEO advice, writing for different demographics and how to best position your brand.

Tips, formulas, templates and examples to help you refine daggy, outdated communications and start grabbing the attention of your new customers or clients.

Ideal for business owners and marketing professionals, Potent: improve your website with powerful copywriting will guide you through easy marketing techniques to jazz up your website so it starts working for, and not against, you.

Number one bestseller

As a new release, Potent, shot straight to the top of the Business Writing Skills category and is now an Amazon bestseller!

Tarot For Business

You're tired of working in a business that doesn't feel right. Or, you want to start your own business, but you don't know where to begin.

Imagine having the clarity and confidence you need to succeed in your new venture. With the Tarot for Business book as your guide, you'll be able to make informed decisions about everything from marketing strategies and finances, to hiring employees and setting goals.

Get clear guidance on what's coming up for your business with Tarot for Business! This insightful user guide has both the major and minor arcana card meanings that have been channelled specifically in relation to business and your success!

All your business questions answered with the wisdom of the universe.

Tarot for Business is a handy guidebook that reframes the traditional tarot deck so it pertains to business.

An insightful user guide that has both the major and minor arcana card meanings that have been channelled that are specifically in relation to business and your business's marketing.

Get clear guidance on:
•What marketing activities to do
•What is coming up for your business
•Who is influencing your success
•Your strengths

Written with significantly helpful, positive and uplifting messages, this book is ideal for business owners or those who are looking to start their own business.

Promote Your Spiritual Business

Promote Your Spiritual Business is one of the best marketing books to help businesses, people and services who work in creative, wellness and heart centred industries. The helpful book has a focus on social media marketing but expands into other ways and areas to make the most of low cost options when promoting and advertising your business or service.

Filled with useful and really simple tips and techniques, Promote Your Spiritual Business book will help you rapidly expand your customers and clients. As well as grow your business the way you have always dreamed.

Market your business and services with ease and

a professionalism at a low cost!

This book is an introduction into digital marketing combines a range of fundamental and practical aspects with an overlay of spiritual "hocus pocus" that will get you started in creating a thriving and sustainable business

Although the book discusses techniques from both traditional and digital marketing, Promote Your Spiritual Business is mostly concerned with digital (or online) marketing because a lot of digital marketing is free or relatively inexpensive.

DISCOVER MORE ABOUT VANESSA JONES

www.vanessajonesauthor.com

and discover new releases and free reads by signing up to:

vanessajonesauthor.com/sign-up

ABOUT THE AUTHOR

Vanessa Jones

Vanessa Jones is a professional writer who runs her own copy-writing and marketing business. Vanessa holds an Advanced Diploma of Professional Writing and has previously been awarded a commendation for the Qantas SOYA writing category, winner of National Year of Reading short  story competition, awarded Outstanding Achievement in Writing Poetry at TAFE SA and a Commendation, Melbourne Poet's Union International Poetry Comp. In her role as SA Writers Centre Youth Ambassador, she ran workshops for school students and adults, presented on and chaired writers festival panels and mentored TAFE students. In addition to publishing seven books, Vanessa has written a feature length screenplay and a pilot script looking for homes.

In 2021, she was shortlisted for the Hothouse Screenwriting Residency with Mercury CX.

PRAISE FOR AUTHOR

5.0 out of 5 stars Captivating read
Reviewed in Australia on 20 May 2021

Loved this book from the start to the end, I couldn't put it down. Highly recommend if you enjoy psychological thrillers

- AMANDA

5.0 out of 5 stars Engaging and enjoyable read!
Reviewed in Australia on 27 April 2021

I loved sharing the journey of discovery with Sophie as she unravelled the mystery that was her life. A juicy plot and engaging characters.

- JANINE

Printed in Great Britain
by Amazon